Provincetown Whispers

A Cape Cod Series

Kimberly Thomas

Prologue

Two Months Ago

She pushed herself to her feet and secured the cap on the marker. Tilting her head, she glanced around the room, studying the boxes lined up, all marked in her neat, cursive handwriting.

As she continued to glance around the spacious living room, bathed in warm, buttery hues of yellow, Lily placed a hand over her chest, over the hollow ache that had been there for days. She'd never seen anything sadder nor lonelier than the sight of her living room, empty and devoid of the life it had once held, with nothing but storage boxes containing a lifetime's worth of memories.

For the life of her, she couldn't quite figure out how she'd gotten here.

Or when the knots in her stomach she'd been carrying around for weeks would go away.

Behind her, the front door clicked open, and the

workers, dressed in jeans and old T-shirts, poured back in and glanced at her expectantly. "What else do you need us to move, Mrs. Alrich?"

Lily blinked and looked over at them. "There's still a few more boxes."

The blond man nodded and stood up straighter. "Yes, ma'am. Which ones will you be wanting us to move?"

Lily coughed and glanced back at the boxes, a strange lump rising in the back of her throat. She'd marked the boxes already and had spent days trying to determine which were of any use to her and which would go to a storage unit she'd rented out in the middle of the city.

"The ones marked 'go,'" Lily replied finally. She swallowed past the lump and folded her arms over her chest. "Leave the others, please."

With a sigh, she watched the movers stir, heading toward the remaining boxes. Once they'd moved the last of them, Lily shut the door behind them and spun to face the empty apartment. A warm breeze blew in through the open window, making the hairs on the back of her neck rise. A heaviness settled in the center of her chest as Lily drifted up the stairs toward the rooms.

Slowly, she peeked into one room after the next, shutting the doors behind her as she did. Once she was done upstairs, she made her way back down, the heaviness in her chest growing.

She wandered into the office, paused in the doorway, and glanced around the room where her husband had spent most of his life.

Her now *ex*-husband.

The life they'd built together now seemed like a lifetime ago.

When she pulled the door shut behind her and

drifted back into the living room, tears sprang to Lily's eyes. She remembered the first day Lance had brought her here: fresh out of college, pregnant, and with her whole life ahead of her. She'd been blindfolded then, and Lance's sure and steady hands had held her in place till he removed the blindfold and gestured around him.

Lily would never forget how it had felt to stand in the doorway with an arm draped over her stomach, where a swell of emotion—fear, anxiety, and uncertainty—were fluttering in her chest. She recalled turning to Lance with tears in her eyes and a beaming smile—still thought of how he'd kissed her like the world had been theirs for the taking. A bittersweet feeling settled in the pit of her stomach, reminding her that it hadn't been all bad, despite how it was ending.

She'd been an idiot then, believing they really could have it all.

Had she dreamed too big, reached too high? Was this the price she had to pay?

With a slight shake of her head, Lily rubbed a hand over her face.

All of the taco nights, the family movie nights spent curled up on the couch with Lance while their three children squirmed and argued on the floor underneath them. Lily remembered every dance rehearsal and every dinner she'd slaved over, only to sit around the table afterward, marveling at how she'd gotten so lucky.

It all came back to her, in snippets at first, then all at once, leaving her gasping, the ache in her chest growing stronger.

When, exactly, had her dream life turned into a nightmare?

Try as she might, Lily couldn't pinpoint the exact

moment. All she knew was she'd gone from being married to one of the most eligible men in the city, and hosting some of the most lavish parties, to screaming matches that ended with her berating herself and wondering where it all had gone wrong.

Lance had gone from being the man of her dreams to a complete stranger, seemingly overnight.

But in her heart, she knew it had been a long time coming. Since the birth of their third child, Lauren, she'd felt Lance pulling away, disappointment and frustration etched onto his face whenever he looked at her. She'd fought the feeling. For years, she'd clung to their marriage by the skin of her teeth, and it still hadn't been enough.

You did everything you could, Lily. There was nothing else you could've done, and you know it.

Once upon a time, Lily had imagined a career for herself as a dietician.

She'd given it up to be the wife of a criminal lawyer and raise their three children. Yet, although the life of a socialite and part-time dietician was the only life she'd ever known, Lily was filled with an odd combination of fear and excitement over what the future held for her and the many possibilities it now presented.

Especially now she'd sold her house and was starting over.

You can do this, Lily. Plenty of people start over. And you've got a nice little safety net while you figure things out.

"Hello?"

Lily spun around, jolted out of her memories by the sound of her oldest son's voice. He pushed the front door open with a creak, and his dark hair emerged first, glistening beneath the early morning sun. When Liam stepped into the house, a small smile hovering on the edge of his lips, she was taken aback by how much he looked like his father. Everything from his dark hair and dark eyes to the sure way he held himself reminded her of her ex.

And it sent another knot straight to her stomach.

Liam stepped forward and pulled her in for a hug. "I figured you'd need the company."

"Thank you, sweetheart." Lily clung to him for a little longer, allowing the familiar scent of his spicy aftershave to wash over her. "You didn't have to come all the way out here."

Liam drew back and smiled. "I wanted to. Besides, I stopped by and got us some coffee on the way."

Lily's lips curved into a smile. "That smells delicious."

Liam placed her hand into the crook of his elbow and led her to the marble kitchen table. He pulled out a stool for her and waited till she sat down. Once she did, he set down his own cup and leaned over the counter. In silence, she sipped on her coffee and studied him.

Where had all the time gone?

In the blink of an eye, Liam had gone from wanting to cuddle up to her on the couch and play with his action figures to being on track to become a criminal lawyer, just like his father.

When he looked over at her, Lily saw the concern and worry written in the depths of his eyes and straightened. "I'm fine."

Liam eyed her over the rim of his cup. "You know it's okay if you aren't. This is a big step."

Lily nodded and took a long sip of her drink, the liquid burning a path down her throat before settling in her stomach. "I know it is."

"I'm sure you could buy the house back if you wanted," Liam added, his eyes moving steadily over her face. "I don't think the new owners will care since they want to tear it down and rebuild."

Lily sighed and reached between them. She placed her hand on top of Liam's and squeezed. "I can't live here, sweetheart. What good would it do me?"

With memories around every corner and the weight of her failed marriage lingering in all the nooks and crannies...

Lily had loved her home and had poured a lot of time, energy, and sweat into the two-story Victorian house.

Now, she couldn't imagine spending one more minute there.

Liam nodded and cleared his throat. "Okay."

Lily gave his hand another squeeze. "I know this is hard for you too. It's the house where you and your siblings grew up, but you'll always have the memories."

Liam studied her face, a furrow appearing between his brows. "Are you sure you don't want to come and stay with me?"

"Absolutely." Lily drew her hand back and sat up straighter. "You and Laura are planning a wedding, sweetheart. I don't want to get in the way of that."

"You wouldn't be getting in the way. We'd love your help."

"I've got my own plans, remember?"

Liam finished the last of his coffee and sat the empty cup down. "I still can't believe you're actually going through with this. What if you don't like it there?"

"Then I'll come back."

Liam pushed himself off the counter and ran a hand over his face. "It's a lot of changes, Mom. First, selling the house and now going to Provincetown for a few months?"

Carefully, Lily stood up and smoothed out the front of her shirt. "I know it's a lot of changes, but it feels like the right thing to do."

Liam snorted. "Going off to a town in the middle of an island to meet a family who's never taken an interest in you?"

"That's not their fault; you know that."

Liam blew out a breath. "Yeah, but it's too many changes, too fast."

"It's going to take some time to adapt, but I've spoken to your aunt Heather, and she's helped me make all of the arrangements. I can't wait to meet everyone."

"Aren't you worried they won't be what you expect?"

Lily chuckled. "I'm sure it'll be fine, sweetheart. And I think you'll love them too once you meet them."

Liam muttered something under his breath, too unintelligible for her to discern.

Meeting her mom's side of the family was a big deal, far bigger than she was willing to let on. Lily had spent weeks agonizing over the decision and wondering if it was the right call to make, considering they were nothing but strangers to her. However, after being given a box full of letters written by her late mother and aunt, she felt compelled to seek them out.

After a lifetime of wondering, she was finally getting to meet her mother's family.

Her teenage self would've been thrilled.

"You worry too much, sweetheart," Lily added after a lengthy pause. "I'll be fine, and we'll talk every day."

Liam exhaled and straightened his shoulders. "Okay, fine. I can see I'm not going to get anywhere here, and I know you know what you're doing, so I'll let it go for now. I've got to get to work. Text me later?"

Lily drew him into another hug. "I will. Drive safely."

"I will. Love you."

"Love you too."

As soon as he'd left, Lily grabbed her purse and rummaged through it. She wandered through the house one final time, the memories overwhelming her as she did. She saw herself sitting across from her kids at the breakfast table, with sleep still in her eyes and the sound of their babbling and laughter filling the air. Then she saw them playing on the carpet in the living room while she called out to Lance, her face hurting from smiling so much. She saw a younger version of herself and Lance dancing by the light of the refrigerator while the kids slept soundly.

All of those Christmases, all of the birthdays, and all of the holidays.

The four walls of their home held so much life, and they had so many stories to tell.

Lily almost couldn't bear the thought of saying goodbye, although she knew she had to.

This time, when she went back downstairs, her steps were slower and less certain, and she had a large lump in her throat.

In the doorway to the house, she paused and took the envelope out of her purse. Inside, she had all of the contact information and a detailed itinerary for her time in Provincetown, Massachusetts.

She fingered the envelope and thought of her aunt Mae.

Darling Aunt Mae, who had reached out a month prior upon seeing the news of Lily's divorce splashed all over the society papers. Lily hadn't known what to expect when her estranged aunt reached out. However, the last thing she'd anticipated was her father's sister revealing her father and stepmother had been feeding Lily lies to keep the truth about her mother under wraps, ever since she'd been a child.

According to Mae, her mother had been a wonderful woman, one her father had never deserved.

By the end of the meeting, Mae had pulled out a package full of envelopes written by her mother's sister, Aunt Heather. The very same aunt she was to meet for the first time.

It was all so very strange.

Lily hadn't been able to go through the letters while sitting in the middle of a crowded café in a busy part of the city. Instead, she'd taken the letters home and waited until she was sitting on the floor of their home, half-empty boxes surrounding her, to rip one open.

Since then, she hadn't looked back.

Lily flipped the lights off, stepped outside, and slammed the door shut behind her.

She didn't want to look back anymore, only forward. It was time for a new chapter in her life.

Chapter One

Lily had the windows rolled down, allowing the sickly sweet smell of wildflowers to waft into her car. With the music turned down and nothing but the open road for miles ahead, she relaxed against her seat. Trees whipped past on both sides, leaves and grass peppered with the wide array of flowers in full bloom.

After a long and trying winter, spring was finally here.

With a sigh, she turned the music down further and gripped the steering wheel with both hands. On the passenger seat next to her was the box full of letters her aunt Heather had written to her every year since her mother had died, up until Liam's birth.

There was an entire world in those pages, the secret having been within Lily's reach all along. She kept one hand on the steering wheel, the other touching the top of the closed box, as if to assure herself it was still there.

Driving from New York to Falmouth had been Lily's idea, giving her four hours to adapt to the idea of leaving behind the only life she'd ever known.

Taking the scenic route had seemed like a good decision at the time. Now, she had no idea if she could bear to be alone with her thoughts for that long. Not when she kept turning over everything she knew about her mother, from the fact she'd abandoned Lily when she was barely a year old to the fact she'd died tragically when Lily was only six. She could fit everything she knew about her mother in one hand and had long since made her peace with her ignorance.

Or so she'd thought.

Aunt Heather had proven that Lily only succeeded in pushing it down.

One particular letter came to mind, written after Liam was born. The pages were now worn and crumpled around the edges, but Lily could recite it from memory.

As she settled back against her seat and lowered the music, she smiled to herself.

Dear Lily,

I can't believe you've just had your first child. Your mother would've been so proud of you. Kelly would've loved being a grandmother. She was so warm and caring, and she had so much love to give.

I hope you know that.

I know you've never answered my letters, and a part of me thinks you never will, but I still cling to the hope that it's not too late. You do, after all, have a whole family here that's rooting for you, that's celebrating your successes as their own. We love you so very much, Lily.

And I can't wait to meet my great-nephew.

You're going to make an amazing mom.

With love,
    Aunt Heather

Lily blinked back the tears and returned to the present with a jolt. She maintained her viselike grip on the steering wheel, some of the knots in her stomach unfurling.

For years, she'd believed every lie spoon-fed to her by her father and stepmother, allowing their hate and biases to color her opinion of her mother and her mother's family. She'd even been told her mother's family wanted nothing to do with her.

Why had she taken everything they said at face value?

Why hadn't she known any better?

Her phone rang, interrupting her train of thought.

Her daughter's name flashed across the car screen, bringing a smile to her lips. "Hi, honey."

"Sounds like you're on the road already," Sara commented; Lily could practically hear the smile in her voice. "How's the road trip going?"

"I miss you all already."

Sara laughed. "You can't miss us *that* badly since you're going all the way to... What was it again?"

"I'll be headed to Falmouth first, then I'll make my way to Provincetown." Lily chuckled. "I'm glad to know you listen carefully when I talk."

"I *do* listen," Sara insisted, her voice growing muffled

before returning in full force. "It's just a lot of names to remember."

"Some family members live in Falmouth, and some of them live in Provincetown."

"And you're going to be staying in Falmouth first, right?"

Lily nodded. "I'll be staying in a hotel Aunt Heather booked for me. While I'm there, I'll get to know the side of the family that lives in Falmouth."

"Remind me again why you're staying in a hotel. They're your mom's family, right?"

"Because I hardly know them," Lily reminded her, pausing to check the rearview mirror. "How would you feel about a relative you barely know imposing?"

"I'll let you know if I'm ever in that situation."

"Hopefully, that never happens. Anyway, I thought it would be a good idea for me to stay in a hotel to take some of the pressure off."

"Actually, you might be onto something."

"Your mom does occasionally have good ideas," Lily teased.

"So, Falmouth is where your grandma and grandpa live, right?"

"That's right. Aunt Ashley and Uncle Frankie live there too."

Sara released a deep breath. "That's a lot of relatives. You mentioned something about a Stu guy. Is he another uncle?"

Lily cleared her throat. "Stu is my stepfather. He was married to my...to Kelly."

Sara said something to someone in the background. Then her voice came back on, quieter than before. "Are you sure you want to meet him? You know, it's okay if you don't."

"I want to."

"You sure? Meeting him and his children... That's a lot to take in, Mom. I'm not trying to discourage you or anything. I just think you should slow down."

"Have you been talking to Liam about this?"

Sara paused. "We've all been talking about it. We just want to be sure you're meeting them for the right reasons and not, you know."

"How's Jake? How are his studies?"

"Same old," Sara replied after a brief pause. "You know how Jake is around exam time."

"Mm-hmm."

"Are you mad at me?"

Lily stared at the empty road ahead and ignored the twinge in her stomach. "I'm not using them as a distraction if that's what you're asking."

Sara sighed. "I know that, Mom. But do *they* know that?"

Overnight, Lily had gone from not knowing her birth mother and having no memories of her to discovering a whole other family who had been kept from her. Not only was she driving to Falmouth to meet the grandparents she'd never known, but there was also a slew of aunts and uncles she'd heard nothing of.

Nothing, however, scared her as much as meeting her stepfather and his children. Her half siblings.

No matter what she told her own kids, the thought of meeting the twins, two people with lives of their own who had gotten Kelly to themselves, left a hollow ache in the center of her chest. While she knew neither of them was responsible for how Kelly had abandoned her as a child, a part of her couldn't help but wonder what she'd done wrong—why they were so different.

Why had Kelly left her to start a whole new life?

And why wasn't Lily a part of it?

Since learning of her mother's family, Lily had wondered about the same thing over and over, but each time she came close to voicing her concerns, she backed out. Considering how everyone was just getting to know each other, the last thing she wanted was to cast a dark shadow of doubt and suspicion over everything. No matter how badly she wanted the answers.

"I didn't mean to upset you," Sara continued, now louder. "I just think it's a lot, that's all, but you know I support you regardless."

"Good."

"So, tell me again: Your grandparents live in Falmouth, along with Aunt Heather, Aunt Ashley, and Uncle Frank—"

"Aunt Heather lives in Provincetown, and so does Aunt Rebecca."

"Heather is the one who wrote you all those letters, right?"

"That's the one."

Sara paused. "Is she the retired nurse who's married to Ed, the real estate agent?"

"I'm glad to see you've been paying some attention." Lily switched on the turn signal and took a hard right, pausing to wipe the beads of sweat off of her face. "Heather is married to Ed, and they have two kids: Tammy and Luke."

"Those are your cousins?"

"That's right. They're both married with kids."

"How are you keeping track of all of this?"

16

"Honestly? I made a spreadsheet."

Sara burst into laughter, and Lily immediately brightened at the sound, missing her oldest daughter and wishing she was there next to her. "Maybe you should color code or something to help you differentiate."

"I should," Lily agreed, relaxing her grip on the wheel. "I'm hoping it'll be easier once I start putting faces to the names."

"What about Aunt...Ashley, was it? Is she married too?"

"Yes, and she also has kids who have kids."

Sara blew out a breath. "So, you've got a lot of first cousins, and a lot of first cousins...once removed?"

"It's a lot to process," Lily told her. She reached for the water bottle she kept on the passenger seat and lifted it to her lips. "Maybe I'd better send you the spreadsheet."

Sara snorted. "Yeah, I don't think that's a good idea. I'm getting a headache just thinking about it."

"Well, you have to brush up on the Wilson family tree at some point. Because I want you all to come out to meet them when you can."

"Maybe everyone can wear name cards. Okay, let me see if I remember this right; that leaves Aunt Rebecca, right? She's the one who runs that inn with the funny name."

"The Herring Cove Inn," Lily corrected with a smile. "It's not a funny name. I think it's charming."

"I think it sounds like some kind of venereal disease you'd avoid talking about."

"Be nice," Lily scolded. "You better not make that comment to your great-aunt Rebecca."

"I'll try, but I can't make any promises. Does Aunt Rebecca have kids too?"

"Yes, she does."

Lily heard something ripping, followed by a loud crunching sound. "So, everyone, with the exception of my grandparents, Uncle Frank and Aunt Ashley, live in Provincetown? And Provincetown is where the Herring Cove Inn and Café is situated, right?"

Lily nodded. "Yeah, it's a lot to remember, but I'm basically going to Falmouth first since it's easier to get there by car. After I stay there for a few days, I'll make my way to Provincetown."

"So, you've decided to take them up on the offer to stay in the beach house?"

Lily ran a hand over her face and drank more water. "I think it'll be a good opportunity for me to get to know them better, and what better way to do that than by staying in the beach house?"

"I guess that's one way to do it."

"I'm not having a midlife crisis."

"I didn't say you were," Sara muttered. "I mean, I was thinking it, but you're the one who said it."

"Sweetheart, I know the past few months have been difficult, but this is exactly the kind of change I need. This is going to be a good thing."

"I hope you're right, Mom."

Lily hoped she was right too.

Because it felt like this was her second act in life, and she didn't want to mess it up.

Chapter Two

"You do realize I'm the mom in this scenario, right?" Lily kicked the car door shut with the back of her leg and straightened her back. Having arrived at Falmouth half an hour ago, she had since been bombarded with a swarm of messages from her children, culminating in Liam's phone call. She switched the phone to her other ear and went around to the trunk. After hoisting her bag up, she set it down on the asphalt parking lot and glanced around. "I can manage just fine, Liam."

Situated in the middle of the town, the hotel offered a picturesque and idyllic view of the water and was within walking distance of many restaurants. On her way past, Lily had taken stock of the townspeople, most of them dressed in shorts and T-shirts, and many of whom walked everywhere. Falmouth was much quieter than anticipated, but it was still teeming and bustling with life and colors.

She had taken a few extra turns before driving to the hotel, hoping to get a better feel for the place. Everywhere she looked, greenery was set against a backdrop of gray skies. When she squinted into the distance and saw a few smaller boats bobbing on the water's edge, she breathed a sigh of relief.

"Liam, I'm going to call you later. I want to get settled," Lily interrupted with a shake of her head.

She wheeled her suitcase behind her, the sound loud and jarring against the silence. In the distance, there was a low chirping sound Lily didn't recognize. She ended the call, climbed a small flight of stairs, and pushed the double doors open.

As soon as she did, she glanced around, taking in the hardwood floors, the glistening chandelier, and the big windows offering a clear view of the water in the distance. With a smile, she wheeled her bag behind her and came to a stop on the other side of a desk, where a silver-haired woman sat behind it. She rose to her feet, smoothed out her skirt, and beamed.

"Hi there, welcome to the Falmouth Hotel. How can I help you today?"

Lily leaned against the counter and took out her phone. "Hi, I've got a reservation under the name Lily Alrich."

"Welcome, Ms. Alrich. My name is Dorothy Samuels. Everyone round here calls me Dot. Hold on while I check your reservation."

Her fingers moved over the keyboard at a leisurely pace. Lily spun and cast another look around, spotting a door left ajar leading into an airy, well-lit ballroom and another door that led into a restaurant filled with tables and customers waiting for their food.

"Here we are. Reservation under Ms. Lily Alrich." Dorothy smiled and opened a drawer. She handed Lily a key. "I'm afraid dinnertime is almost over, but there are a few restaurants that are open till later."

"Thank you. I'll manage."

Dorothy nodded. "Your room is on the second floor, down the hallway and to the right. If you need anything, please let me know."

Lily gave her another smile before she took her bag and wheeled it behind her. In the elevator, she stared at her reflection in the glass and paused to run her fingers through her wavy brown hair. Then she touched the dark circles under her eyes and exhaled. As soon as the elevator doors pinged open, she stepped out into a carpeted, cream-colored hallway.

The door to her room clicked open, and she paused in the doorway, groping for the lights. After setting her bag down by the door, Lily wandered into the bathroom and flipped another light on. She stopped in front of the sink, raked her fingers through her hair, and splashed cold water on her face. Then she pulled the bathroom door shut behind her and went back to the front door.

On her way out of the hotel, she felt several pairs of eyes on her, but when she glanced up, no one was looking at her. She shook her head, got into her car, and used her phone to navigate, pulling up on the other side of town in a residential area filled with two-story houses. All of them had front lawns and small driveways.

Lily switched off the engine and leaned forward, gawking at the elegant, polished manor before her with its sprawling lush, green lawn, a white wraparound porch, a gabled roof, and a gravel path that led into a driveway with a small water fountain in the center.

Her grandparents had great taste, selecting a property

that gave them an unobstructed view of Falmouth's inner harbor.

With a smile and a slight thudding of her heart, Lily pushed the car door open and stepped out. The double doors to the manor creaked open, and a couple stepped out, dressed identically in warm colors and with streaks of silver in their hair.

Lily held her breath and covered the distance between them. "You must be Jennifer and Frank Wilson."

Jennifer pulled Lily into a hug and didn't let go for several long moments. "You have no idea how much we've looked forward to this day, sweetie. We've been waiting for years."

Frank pulled her into a hug as soon as his wife was done. "You look so much like our dear Kelly. It's nice to finally meet you, Lily."

Lily pulled away. "Thank you for inviting me."

"Stu is inside, but he didn't want to intrude," Jennifer told her, pausing to give her a maternal smile. "I hope that's okay. I told him we would check with you first."

Lily's stomach gave an odd little lurch. "Yes, of course. I'd like to meet him."

In silence, her grandparents led her back into the house, down a dimly lit hallway that opened into a spacious living room with a brown leather sofa set, pictures on the mantle above the fire, and an open-floor kitchen. A red-haired man sat on one of the couches, tapping his jean-clad leg impatiently. As soon as he saw her, he stood up, and she saw the laugh lines on his face.

She couldn't believe she was meeting her stepfather in person.

It all felt so surreal, like if she reached out and pinched herself, she was going to wake up in a rental a block away from her old house with a strange fluttering in the center of her chest.

"It's so nice to meet you, Lily," Stu said with a smile. "Thank you for agreeing to see me."

Lily nodded and gave him a firm shake. "Of course."

The glass doors slid open, and two more people came in, sporting identical red hair and green eyes and dressed in jeans and T-shirts. Once they saw her, they both moved closer and came to a pause.

Lily glanced between the two of them. "You must be Ian and Sophia. I've heard so much about the two of you. I feel like I know you both already."

Sophia stepped forward and reached for Lily's hand. "We're really happy we're finally meeting you, Lily. I've always wanted a sister."

After weeks of trying to envision it all, it was nothing at all like she expected.

It was better.

She couldn't believe she was finally here or that she was getting to meet with the family she'd never known, the kind she'd dreamed of having as a little girl. Having spent most of her childhood with silence, disapproval, and criticism around every corner, she couldn't wait to see what it felt like to have the opposite.

Impatience, joy, and hope all grew within her.

When her grandparents suggested a walk, Lily jumped at the chance. The sun was beginning to set outside, bathing the world in hues of pink and purple. Lily slowed her pace and shoved both hands into her pockets. She inhaled, the salty, sweet smell of the water already making her feel better. In silence, they continued to walk the grounds near the water's edge.

"You must never get tired of this view," Lily commented. "I don't think I would."

Her grandparents exchanged a quick look. "We have more than enough room if you change your mind about staying with us. One of them even has the same exact view from the window."

Lily wrenched her gaze away from the harbor and the boats lined up on either side of the slow, peaceful waves. "That's very generous, but I don't want to impose."

"You wouldn't be imposing," Jennifer insisted, her eyes alight with pleasure. "We'd love to have you here. You can even stay in Kelly's old room."

"Thank you, but I think it's better if I stay in the hotel while we get to know each other."

"But we're family, and—"

Frank reached for Jennifer's hand and cleared his throat. "We're all just so happy you've found us after all this time. We were hoping you would. Your mother would've been so happy you found your way here."

A lump rose in Lily's throat. "What was she like?"

"She was so full of life," Jennifer whispered after a quick look around her. "And so full of energy. We always said that out of all of our children, she was going to be the one to change the world. She wanted to be the president, you know."

Lily's lips lifted into a smile. "Really?"

Frank nodded. "Oh, yes, and a doctor and a teacher. Kelly wanted to be a lot of things. And we did encourage her to dream big."

"What was the last thing she wanted to be?"

"A vet," Jennifer replied, her shoes crunching against the gravel beneath her. "But I think she couldn't stand the idea of having to put any animals down, so she changed her mind."

Lily nodded, her stomach dipping at the mere mention of her mom.

She wasn't used to hearing her mom being discussed so openly or so lovingly, and it left a warm feeling in the center of her stomach.

Her grandmother stopped and reached for Lily's hands, taking them both into her warm, calloused ones. "We never forgot about you, Lily. We reached out so many times, and we wanted to have a relationship with you, but your father wouldn't let us."

Lily sucked in a harsh breath, her pulse quickening. "I still can't believe he was capable of such a thing."

Her grandfather came to stand next to her grandmother and nodded solemnly. A few feet behind them, Stu, Ian, and Sophia trailed, giving them a wide berth. In the distance, Lily heard the roar of a car, followed by a dog barking.

She studied her grandparents by the sun's dying light and tried to make sense of the jumble of emotions she felt.

Why would her father keep them away from her?

He had known how much it hurt her to know they were out there and didn't care.

"I don't know why he did what he did," her grandfather continued, his expression growing anxious as he wrung his hands together, a shadow settling over his face. "We wanted to believe he had a good reason, but we couldn't find one that made any sense. Your father is a very powerful man, as you know, and he made it clear if we continued to try and reach out to you against his wishes, he was going to make life very difficult for us. He had a lot of control."

None of them were telling her anything she didn't already know.

She'd spent years trying to block out the truth, to make her peace with it.

But Lily was no longer sure she could, not when the exterior he'd worked hard to build was finally cracking, revealing the troubled and cruel man underneath.

How did her father look at himself in the mirror?

How did he justify the lies he'd told to his own flesh and blood?

In a daze, Lily took a step back. "He *is* friends with a lot of powerful people. I just don't understand why he'd lie and keep all of you away from me."

Yet, it sounded exactly like the sort of cruel, manipulative thing he would do.

She'd spent a lifetime making excuses for him and trying to turn the other cheek, but she wasn't sure she could continue to do it.

Not anymore.

"Anyway, there will be plenty of time to talk about everything." Her grandmother draped an arm over her shoulders and steered her back in the direction of the house. "I hope you're hungry because I've made plenty of food."

* * *

After dinner, Lily excused herself and drove back to the hotel, her mind spinning with information. As soon as she stepped in through the front door, her phone buzzed. Lauren's name flashed across the screen, bringing a smile to Lily's lips.

"How's it going? How's everything?"

Lily switched the phone to her other ear. "I should be asking you that. Are you settling in okay at school? How's everything in Chicago?"

"Busy," Lauren replied. "I don't know how you did it, Mom. All of the courses look really hard."

Lily kicked off her shoes and sank onto the bed. "I'm sure you'll do just fine."

"We could open up our own practice when I'm done so we can both be clinic dieticians together."

Lily laughed. "I'd like that."

"Anyway, I know it's been a long day, and you probably want to get some rest. I just wanted to check in. I'll call you tomorrow."

"Okay, be safe. I love you."

"Love you too."

After a quick, hot shower, during which Lily thought of her life in New York, of the endless stream of dinners and parties she hosted, she climbed into bed and stared at the unfamiliar ceiling. Her life in New York felt so far away, and she felt so far removed it might as well have been another life.

The realization left her with a bittersweet mixture of feelings: sadness for the chapter in her life she was closing, fear over what lay ahead, and excitement over getting to know her mother's family at long last.

For the first time in a long time, Lily didn't feel like she was going through the motions.

Falmouth and Provincetown might be exactly what she needed after all.

Chapter Three

"How was your night? Did you sleep well?"

Lily smiled at her grandmother, who stood in the doorway to the hotel entrance and adjusted the strap of her purse. "I slept like a baby, thank you."

Her grandmother reached for Lily's hand, her weathered face full of kindness and eyes shining with warmth and humor. "Good. We thought we'd take you on a tour of Falmouth to show you what you've been missing."

Lily glanced between the two of them. "Are you sure I'm not interrupting anything? I could probably manage with a map or something."

Her grandfather brushed her comment away and came to a stop beside her. "Nonsense. We'd love to show you around. You're going to love Falmouth."

"Let's start with lunch at the Pickle Jar."

Lily smiled and looped her arm through her grandmother's. "Lead the way."

Her grandmother kept up a steady stream of conversation during their walk. With the early afternoon sun on their backs and the empty streets of Falmouth ahead of them, there was a lot to see. Staring at the boutiques lined up on either side, many sold clothes and bags made of recycled material. When they came to a stop outside a cream and gray two-story house on the main street, Jennifer proudly gestured to it. Frank pushed the door open and ushered them inside into a spacious, well-lit area with several wooden tables scattered throughout.

Bright sunlight poured in through the glass windows, causing tiny light particles to dance on the hardwood floors. They were greeted with smiles from the waitstaff, who led them to a table in the back, overlooking a window with a glass jar painted onto it, boasting a pickled cucumber and carrot.

Once they were seated, Jennifer pushed her chair closer to Lily's. "Did you know this place has been open for ten years? And they use all-natural ingredients too."

"I love how much history this place has."

Her grandmother nodded and linked her fingers together. "It was one of the reasons why we wanted to move here. We thought the city was too cold and impersonal, and we like how communities are here."

Frank nodded and murmured something to the waitress. "This place is a lot older than we are."

"Neither of you look a day over forty."

Her grandparents burst into laughter and waved a finger at her. Lily felt something warm unfurl low inside of her chest. During lunch, her gaze darted between the two as they talked about gardening, the ease of their life during retirement, and the fact they were both avid walkers.

She sat still, soaking up all the information and wanting more.

Lily was buzzing with so much excitement she was sure they could all tell.

By the time they ushered her back out onto the busy streets and toward the boardwalk along the Coonnamessett River, Lily was even more excited. It glistened and shimmered underneath the afternoon sun, and they paused to admire their surroundings before they continued walking, with her grandparents pausing to point out the ferry moving to and from Martha's Vineyard.

"You should definitely visit the Island while you're here," Grandma Jennifer insisted. "Frank and I have been a few times, and it's always so beautiful this time of year, and there's so much to do."

"You're probably used to all of the hustle and bustle of New York," Frank added with a small smile. "Once the weather is better, you'll find a lot more activities to do around here."

"Like what?"

Frank paused and ran a hand over his face. "Bike rides, fireworks, that sort of thing."

"That sounds amazing."

And exactly the kind of thing she wanted to experience firsthand.

Everything about this place and her mother's family was making her feel warm and welcome and fuzzy inside.

By then, they were approaching Falmouth Heights Beach, which had more than its fair share of visitors and townspeople, all with towels placed on the sand and looking out at the clear, blue waters. Waves lapped and crashed softly against the edge of the sand, filling Lily with a strange sense of peace and calm.

"We should get going so you can meet your uncle,

Frankie," her grandpa Frank, decided with a broad hand gesture. "He works at the real estate company on Commercial Street, and he's really excited to meet you."

"I think it's great that you're able to be so active. It's definitely not this safe in New York."

"It's very safe in Falmouth. Most of us know each other, and we look out for each other," her grandmother replied, pausing to pat her hand. "Come along, dear."

With that, they set off at an even pace, weaving in and out of people to make their way back to the main street. Lily kept glancing around her, trying to take in all of the sights and colors. Once they stopped outside a blue-colored store with large glass windows and a chimney on the roof, Lily gawked.

"This here's Wilson Realty," Frank said, jutting his chest out proudly. "We built it from scratch, and we've got a second office in Provincetown."

"And I can't believe they let family run that one too," a new voice said, belonging to a tall, dark-haired man in dark jeans and a button-down shirt. He stepped outside, and Lily couldn't help but think he was the spitting image of her grandfather, except for the eyes. He took both of Lily's hands in his and gave her a firm shake, making her arms grow sore.

"It's great to meet you, Lily. I'm your uncle Frank, but everybody calls me Frankie. You'll need to stop by for a proper tour sometime," her uncle said with a broad smile. "I'm sure you'll love it."

Lily gave him a smile in return. "I'm sure I will."

Grandma Jen glanced between the two of them and settled on her son, giving him a pointed look. "Don't forget the barbecue starts at four, and don't be late."

"I won't be late, Ma."

"You're always late," Jennifer scolded. "And Lily is looking forward to meeting Paula and the kids."

Uncle Frankie gave her a quick wink. "You're going to love them."

Her grandparents kept up another steady stream of conversation during the walk back to her car. In silence, she drove them all back to her grandparents' house and parked her car in the driveway. As soon as they stepped inside, she went into the kitchen and began to help. Together, all three of them set up the tables outside, unfolded the chairs, and took out the plastic plates.

Stu, Ian, and Sophia arrived first, bringing with them a large heap of fruits and vegetables. Her grandfather and Stu set to work chopping the salad. A short while later, Lucy Dapp, Ian's wife, came in and blew him a kiss before stepping out into the backyard to help out Sophia and her kids, Zac and Zoe. Ian and Lucy's kids, Kelli, Dana, and Dean, arrived next, carrying plastic bags filled with chips, sandwich bread, and soda.

Everyone greeted Lily with warmth and enthusiasm, as if she'd been a part of this all along. Aunt Ashley pulled Lily into a tearful hug when she arrived, pausing to exclaim how much Lily looked like her mother. She draped an arm over her niece's shoulders and tugged her along, introducing her to her husband, Jude, and their three kids, Jeff, Emily, and Tara. Lily figured her aunt was in her late sixties, with her salt-and-pepper hair flowing past her shoulders naturally. Her arms and legs were toned, suggesting Aunt Ashley liked to keep in shape. She was stunning.

Someone handed Lily a glass of lemonade, and she chugged it all, trying to keep all of the names and faces separate in her head. She had the vague sense of being encased in a happy bubble, with more and more relatives showing up until her grandparents' backyard was teeming with people, all of them making easy conversation underneath the midafternoon sun.

Her grandfather stoked the coals and waved to Frank Jr., who came in with sweat on his forehead and a disgruntled-looking Paula by his side. She offered Lily a quick hug before motioning to their kids, Jonathan and Suzie.

Soon, smoke began to rise from the barbecue, and the smell of sizzling meat and chicken filled the air. Aunt Ashley stayed close to Lily's side, making her circle the entire backyard a few times during their introductions. When Lily made her way to the refreshment table, she was introduced to her uncle's grandkids, Jaxon and Suzie, who sat with their feet propped against empty chairs and their phones held up to their faces.

Lily gave them an awkward wave and downed a few more glasses of lemonade.

"There you are." Sophia, her stepsister, draped an arm over her shoulders and led her to a quiet corner where the two of them sat side by side on a swing. "I'm sorry we haven't gotten the chance to talk much."

"There's a lot for us to catch up on." Ian sat down opposite her and kicked his legs out. "Mom died the year after we were born, so we didn't really know her either."

Lily frowned. "I'm sorry."

Sophia sighed. "Dad used to tell us stories about her all the time, and she talked about you, you know. She really wanted us all to meet someday."

"Really?"

"Oh, absolutely. According to Dad, she wanted us to

know all about our sister and how, someday, she was going to come and live with us."

Lily cleared her throat. "I didn't know that."

"We wish we could've known her too," Ian told her, his expression turning solemn. "For what it's worth, I think she would've loved having us all under the same roof."

Lily gave them both a genuine smile. "Thank you. It really means a lot to me to hear you say that."

Because she had spent most of her life thinking her own mother hadn't wanted her, it was more than a little unnerving to realize she had been wrong.

"So, you're off to Provincetown in the morning?"

Lily nodded in Ian's direction. "Yeah, but I'd love it if you two came to visit. We can do some more catching up."

Sophia made a sweeping hand gesture and chuckled. "If you're not overwhelmed by all of this by then, sure."

"It is a little overwhelming," Lily admitted, her eyes sweeping over everyone, letting conversation and laughter rise and fall around her. "But it also feels good."

And her heart felt full.

It had been a long time since she'd felt that, not since her early days of being married to Lance.

"We can make the drive up to Provincetown," Ian added, pausing to rise to his feet. "Let us know when, and we'll make a weekend of it."

"I'd like that." Lily twisted so she was facing Sophia. "What else did Stu say about Ke—our mother?"

"Well, he said she was very warm and loving," Sophia replied, her eyes glistening with tears and her voice growing quiet and thick. "Grandma and Grandpa told us that she used to find joy and hope in everything—a very positive person. I think she really would've loved this."

Lily's throat closed up, and she didn't say anything.

When everyone was called to dinner, Lily found herself seated at a long table, wedged in between her half siblings on one side, her grandparents on the other, and her aunts and uncle opposite her. A steady stream of conversation was maintained as the food was passed around, and laughter filled the air.

When the evening wrapped up and the stars were high in the sky, Lily walked back to her car and spent the ride thinking of her father and how much he'd taken away from her. By the time she pulled up outside the hotel, she had all but convinced herself to confront him, to demand to know why he had kept her mother's family away from her.

She parked the car, walked up the stairs, and made a beeline for the elevator. Once she stepped into her room and flicked on the lights, some of the anger she felt abated. She removed her shoes, left them by the door, and lowered herself onto a chair overlooking the small terrace.

Then she took the picture frame out of her purse and held it up to the fluorescent lighting. It was one of the last pictures ever taken of her mother, and her grandmother had insisted she have it. In the picture, Kelly was in a knee-length blue dress with the Nobska Lighthouse in the background, her beautiful locks flowing out behind her, and a bright smile on her oval face. The longer she studied the picture, the tighter her stomach grew at the thought of her father being able to take all of this away from her without a second thought.

How could he have done this to her?

Lily touched two fingers to the glass frame, a single tear sliding down her cheek. "I wish I could have had the chance to have known you, Mom."

Chapter Four

L ily leaned forward, turned down the volume, and glanced around her.

As she drove through a commercial street with a three-mile spread of art galleries, souvenir shops, and restaurants, she couldn't help but marvel at the unusual architecture around her. From bright cursive signs out front to old Victorian houses, Provincetown had it all.

Situated on the edge of the continent, sixty miles out to sea, there was something in Provincetown for everyone, blending together a unique mix of different cultures and experiences. In the distance, Lily spotted the warm waters of Herring Cove Beach and smiled to herself. In awe, she continued to drive through the narrow streets at a leisurely pace, grinning at the sight of Macmillan Pier, remembering it was home to one of the world's natural deep-water harbors.

Greenery snaked on either side of her, and crystal blue waters glistened underneath the midmorning sun.

Lily squinted and spotted a lighthouse in the middle of the sand dunes, standing tall and proud in spite of its faded paint. She slowed the car to a crawl and came to a stop outside the picturesque, two-story beach house she would be staying at.

Once she killed the engine, Lily peered through the windshield, her sense of awe increasing as it glistened in the sunlight, beckoning her with its charming facade. White clapboard siding adorned the home's exterior, with navy-blue shutters and a sloping gabled roofline that boasted two dormer windows atop the second floor. The home sat atop a gentle slope along the dunes, providing panoramic views of the sparkling water below.

The entire town she'd just driven through was picturesque and idyllic, nothing at all like the hustle and bustle of the concrete jungle that was New York. In Provincetown, everything seemed calmer, especially bathed in warm, buttery hues of gold. The townspeople who wandered the streets looked happy and at peace with the world.

Lily wondered if she was going to feel the same.

With a sigh, she pushed her door open and stepped out, the smell of the saltwater hitting her first. She inhaled, shoved both hands into the pockets of her shorts, and then exhaled as she took in the house. The front of the home had a large wraparound veranda that immediately caught her eye. Made from warm, honey-colored wood, the expansive porch wrapped around the front and side of the home, providing ample space for outdoor entertaining and gorgeous views of the beach and water. Two wooden rocking chairs sat at opposite ends of the porch, inviting visitors to sit and enjoy the sea breeze.

Out of the corner of her eye, she saw a flash of movement, and the door to the house flew open, revealing two women with wavy, auburn hair, brown eyes, and broad smiles. Together, they climbed down the steps and made a beeline for her.

They were identical in their dresses that fell just past their knees, Lily barely had a chance to realize who they were before they engulfed her in a hug. After a brief hesitation, Lily hugged them back and squeezed her eyes shut. One of them, the taller one, drew away first and gave her a watery smile.

"It's so nice to finally meet you, Lily. I'm your aunt Heather."

The woman next to her carried the same distinct almond-shaped eyes, button nose, and heart-shaped face, so she couldn't have been anyone but her other aunt.

Aunt Rebecca sniffed and pulled away to look at her. "Goodness, those tabloids do not do you justice."

"Tabloids?"

Aunt Rebecca took a step back and studied her. "Yes, we've been seeing your pictures all over the tabloids for years. It was the only way we could keep up with you after you got married and moved away."

"You look just like your mother." Aunt Heather held a handout, and Lily took it.

Slowly, Aunt Heather spun her around, commenting on her toned body, shoulder-length brown hair, and her brown, almond-shaped eyes. When she was done, Aunt Heather pulled her in for another hug, squeezing so hard Lily was sure her ribs were going to hurt.

"Heather, you're going to crush the poor girl to death," Aunt Rebecca scolded with a frown. "We don't want her running back to New York."

Abruptly, Aunt Heather released her and sniffed. "I'm sorry. We've just been dreaming about this day for so long. I was beginning to wonder if it was ever going to come."

Lily cleared her throat. "I'm glad I'm finally here."

Aunt Rebecca draped an arm over her shoulders and steered her up the stairs. Lily had to steal a few more glances between the two. They both looked to be in great shape, considering they were well in their seventies. Aunt Heather looked to be around five foot eight, while Aunt Rebecca was around five foot five.

"We have so much catching up to do. Now, tell me; Heather says you're in the health field."

Lily nodded. "Yes, I'm a dietician."

Aunt Rebecca's eyebrows drew together. "Forgive my ignorance, dear. What does a dietician do?"

"Well, I am a health professional who's considered to be an expert in nutrition and human diet. I blend scientific research, nutrition, and behavioral science to promote health, prevent disease, and mold the dietary choices of healthy and sick people."

Aunt Rebecca patted her hand. "That sounds really interesting. Do you have a lot of patients?"

Lily paused. "Not as many as I would like. I didn't get to practice much in New York because of the kids and...Lance."

Aunt Rebecca twisted the knob and pushed the door open. As soon as she stepped inside, Lily came to a complete halt. With tile floors underneath her feet, a veranda that overlooked the ocean, and an open-floor kitchen with modern appliances, the house looked nothing like its exterior. Exchanging quick smiles, her aunts showed her around the rest of the house, from the two rooms downstairs and a smaller connecting bathroom to the three large rooms upstairs, all with clear views of the water.

The entire house had an airy, spacious feel to it, and bathed in the warm hues of the sun, Lily thought she had fallen in love with it already. In silence, the two of them left her in the main bedroom, with its own bathroom and a balcony, in order to unpack. As soon as she came back downstairs, it was Aunt Heather who took Lily's hand and led her outside.

The entire house overlooked the bluff, offering her an unobstructed view of the ocean, the same one she got from her veranda.

Aunt Rebecca came to a stop on the other side of her and made a sweeping hand gesture, the proud smile never leaving her face. "There are more than a few restaurants nearby, and you've got a supermarket. There's also a vet, a few medical practices—"

Aunt Heather pointed into the distance, and her smile grew wider. "And we live just over there. See how close we are?"

Lily glanced between the two of them. "That's great."

She liked knowing they were close as she navigated unfamiliar terrain. They had been so warm and welcoming already. Together, the two of them led her up to the house and settled on the back veranda that overlooked the water. Aunt Heather retrieved a pitcher of iced lemonade from the fridge and poured them all a generous amount.

"This place is beautiful," Lily murmured before setting her drink back down. "How come no one stays here?"

"Your mom used to love coming up here," Aunt Rebecca replied in between sips of her drink. She tucked a blond lock behind her ear before continuing, "We thought you'd love it too, and you're welcome to stay as long as you like."

Aunt Heather looked over at her, her eyes wide and full of emotion. Her voice trembled a little, so she stopped to clear her throat several times. "We actually hope you'll be staying permanently, but we don't want to put any pressure on you or anything. It's completely up to you."

Aunt Rebecca set down her drink and gave her sister an exasperated look. "I thought we agreed we were going to give her some space to adjust to everything before we told her. You'll have to excuse Heather, Lily; she doesn't get out much."

Aunt Heather sputtered and shot her sister a withering look.

Lily chuckled and hid her expression behind her drink.

Already, she could imagine herself staying there, eating her meals on the veranda by the water, biking the steep grades and sharp turns of the Province Lands bike trail. She could even see herself on her morning runs, winding through the narrow but colorful streets of the town. Although she hadn't allowed herself to think of the next step, Lily had considered what it would be like to have her own clinic. She could dedicate even more of herself to the field.

Aunt Rebecca leaned forward and patted her hand, a soft smile hovering on the edge of her lips. "Why don't we show you where everything is before we go into town? You can see the café and inn."

Lily finished her drink and stood up.

Laughing, her aunts led her back into the house. Aunt Rebecca opened and closed several cupboards while Aunt Heather stood in the middle of the living room, trying to fix her graying brunette hair in a bun at the nape of her neck. Once they were done, they took her back upstairs, and she got a closer look at the other rooms, seeing a brief image of her children there, filling the house with love and laughter. With a smile, she followed her aunts back downstairs, pausing in the doorway to get her purse and a sweater.

Outside, a warm breeze drifted past them, and Lily enjoyed the sun's warmth on the back of her neck. Her shoes crunched against the gravel underneath her. Her aunts walked on either side, pointing out everything from the beach to the towering pilgrim monument, nestled in the middle of town and offering a bird's eye view of the historic city.

She felt like everywhere she looked, she could see the water.

The houses gave way to restaurants and souvenir shops, and nestled on the outskirts of Commercial Street sat the Herring Cove Inn and Café. Lily's eyes moved over the large windows and cream-colored exterior, and she watched a steady stream of people coming in and out of the café. Upon closer inspection, she realized the café itself offered another view of the water, the town's best feature by far.

Her aunts led her into the inn, past the front desk, where Aunt Rebecca's daughter-in-law, Alice, sat. She offered them all an enthusiastic wave as they walked through the double doors of the kitchen.

"Everyone, this is Lily Alrich, Kelly's daughter."

A chorus of greetings rose through the air, and Lily gave them all a small wave.

"Lily, this is the staff of Herring Cove Inn and Café. We're all like family here, so it won't be long before you get to know each and every one of them."

Lily twisted to face Aunt Rebecca. "You run the inn, right?"

"That's right, honey. And Aunt Heather is the one who runs Wilson Real Estate's Provincetown branch. Think of it as the 'brunette' runs the inn, and the 'blonde' runs the real estate office."

Aunt Heather threw her head back and laughed. "That's one way to describe it. Ed, my husband, and I run the real estate office, but he's running some errands. You'll get to meet him later. You'll also meet Tammy and Luke, who also work at the real estate office."

Lily's mind spun and raced, trying to sort through and process all of the names and faces. "It must be tricky having your kids work with you."

With so many people to remember and so much catching up to do, the last thing she wanted was to disappoint anyone.

Lily's stomach was already full of anxious butterflies.

Aunt Heather smiled. "We all manage. Angie, come over here and meet your cousin. Lily, this is your cousin, Angie. She's the chef here at the Herring Cove Inn."

Angie draped a rag over her shoulders and stuck her hand out. "It's nice to finally meet you, cousin."

After another round of introductions, Heather and Lily walked arm in arm toward Aunt Heather's house a few blocks away from Commercial Street. There, Lily helped Heather and Aunt Rebecca set up for supper, setting out plates and counting out drinks. When the sun dipped below the horizon, everyone began to arrive, starting with Aunt Heather's husband, Uncle Ed, and their two kids, Tammy and Luke. Tammy introduced her husband, James, and their two kids, Abby and Tania.

Her cousin, Luke, on the other hand, was married to Denise and waved over their kids, Josh and Emma. When Cousin Angie came in, she gave Lily a friendly smile and drifted off, leaving Lily to meet her siblings, Rob and Terry. Terry was a widow with two sullen teenagers, Ron and Glen Jr., who grunted in greeting. As soon as Alice spotted Lily from the distance and waved her over, Lily wandered there and saw her Aunt Rebecca's daughter-in-law signaling to her husband, Rob, and their son, Charlie.

At the end of the night, after a hearty supper and easy conversation, Lily walked back to the beach house with a warm feeling in the center of her stomach. As soon as she shut the door behind her, Liam called, his voice sounding lighter than she'd heard it in a while.

"How's everything going?"

"I met the rest of the family tonight," Lily replied, pausing to leave her shoes by the door. "They're all so lovely, Liam. You'll really like them."

"You sound exhausted."

"It's been a lot," Lily responded, slowly climbing up the stairs. "How's work? And how's Laura?"

"Wedding planning is driving her crazy. You know what a perfectionist she is."

Lily pushed the door to her room open and stepped in. "You'll let me know if either of you need any help, okay?"

"We will," Liam promised. "So, tell me about everyone. What's the house like? Is Provincetown as beautiful as they say?"

Lily explained her day and then said goodnight to her son. It was a long, exhausting day, but one that was full of love and had no regrets. She was excited to see what would happen next.

Chapter Five

Bright sunlight flooded her room and danced behind her eyelids.

Lily pried one eye open, then the other, and blinked, her vision swimming in and out of focus. Once her gaze sharpened and she glanced around, confusion filled her at the unfamiliar room. Then, the previous day's events came back, slowly at first, then all at once.

The Herring Cove Beach house was beautiful in the morning.

With a smile, she threw the covers off and padded into the bathroom. There, she took a hot shower and studied her reflection in the mirror. With wavy brown hair that fell just past her shoulders, brown eyes, and a figure she kept as slim and athletic as possible with constant exercise and watching what she ate, Lily thought she looked quite good for her age. At forty-nine, she had to work hard to stay in shape, especially with her declining metabolism, but she was proud of herself.

Lily was startled to realize she saw the similarities between herself and her mother. After years of wondering, she saw she and her mother shared the same height and the same narrow waist and round hips.

The thought brought a smile to her face.

When she emerged in a pair of shorts and a T-shirt, it felt like she was ready to take the day on. Imbued with an unfamiliar energy and with a spring in her step, she took another stroll through the house, pausing at the pictures on the wall leading downstairs.

Many of them were of her aunts, posing in different parts of the town or along the beach.

She touched the pictures of her mother, an ache settling in the middle of her chest. Her heart gave an odd little twist when she spotted the picture of Kelly on the back veranda with the water behind her and a glorious smile on her face.

It was how she had imagined her mother, happy and carefree.

Lily's smile slipped as she made her way downstairs and into the kitchen. After whisking two eggs and chopping up a few vegetables, she heated up a pan. Then she waited for the eggs to sizzle and leaned over the marble kitchen counter. She was washing the dishes and marveling at the view from her kitchen window when her phone rang.

Dread settled in the pit of her stomach when she saw her father's name.

Lily sucked in a harsh breath and pressed the phone to her ear. "Hello?"

"How dare you? How dare you go to Provincetown to meet your mother's family? How dare you believe the lies coming out of that woman's mouth?" he hissed through the line.

"How dare I? *How dare I?* For the past few days, I've

been in Cape Cod, getting to know my mother's family, and *you're* the one who's upset?" she blurted right back.

Eric released an angry breath. "Of course, I'm upset. I had to learn about this from your siblings, who are furious too, by the way."

"Don't bring them into this," Lily snapped, pausing to run her fingers through her hair. "You're the one who's at fault here, Dad. I don't even know what to say to you."

"I don't know what lies Mae's been telling—"

"Don't talk about Aunt Mae like that," Lily interrupted with a lift of her chin. "At least she told me the truth. You've been lying to me my whole life."

Silence stretched between them.

Lily stepped away from the sink and swallowed. "So, it is true. All those lies, all those stories you spun about my mother...none of it was real, was it?"

Eric made a low, angry sound and then fell silent.

"You know what? I've spent the past few days trying to figure out why and trying to defend you, but I can't. I can't do this right now."

Without waiting for a response, Lily ended the call and shoved the phone into her pocket. Her hands were trembling when she cupped them together and placed them under the faucet. She splashed cold water on her face before gripping the sink. After several deep breaths, she pushed herself away from the sink and glanced around the house.

How could her own father have kept this from her?

Her entire life, she'd been told a story, one Eric had woven to keep the truth away from her. Lily had always known her father had a mean and cruel streak, one she'd worked hard to avoid, but she couldn't justify him keeping her mother away from her. Rather than telling her the truth, he'd behaved horribly, painting her mother as the villain all along.

How many of his family members already knew this?

How many had looked her in the eye and kept it to themselves?

With a slight shake of her head, Lily stepped out of the kitchen and into the living room. She snatched her keys off the table behind the door and hurried outside. With a cool, brisk wind on her face and the warmth of the sun on her back, she set off at a leisurely pace, taking the walking path she'd noticed earlier, one that led directly to the beach.

The entire time, her heart didn't stop pounding, and she couldn't shake off the nausea that kept rising in her throat. Each step, each breath brought back the memories of all those years she'd curl up by a window and cry out for her mother. Of all the times her father had looked her in the eye and spun his tales. Her entire life, she'd been told she was an accident, that Kelly hadn't been looking to have kids when she had her.

Lily had even convinced herself that her mother had done her a favor by leaving her behind. It had been difficult to reconcile herself to that, especially at the tender age of five, but she hadn't been given much of a choice. Her father had even gone so far as to convince Lily that Kelly hadn't wanted to hear from either of them.

She remembered being horrified at the realization.

Abruptly, Lily came to a stop at the bottom of the path and placed one hand on either side of her thighs. The blood was roaring in her ears, and she could barely breathe or hear anything past the uneasy hammering inside of her chest. Over and over, she heard her father's callous, hard voice inside her head, reminding her of the burden she was.

The more she thought about it, the worse she felt.

How could her own father have been such a monster?

Tears burned the back of her eyes as Lily descended the few remaining steps and stepped onto the beach. In a daze, she lowered herself onto the warm sand and drew her knees up to her chest. Other than a few other locals, the beach was mostly empty, allowing Lily to stare straight ahead and sort through her thoughts.

A golden retriever bounded up to her and sat down in front of her. He barked, wagged his tail, and tilted his head at her.

Lily reached a hand out, and he shoved his nose into it. When his tongue darted out to lick her palm, Lily's mouth lifted into the ghost of a smile. Out of the corner of her eye, she saw a flash of movement, and a familiar figure approached in the distance. Once the figure moved closer, Lily recognized her aunt Rebecca, hair pinned on top of her head and dressed in a pair of colorful pants and billowing top.

"Mind if I sit?"

Lily shook her head and stretched her legs out in front of her. "Not at all."

Slowly, Rebecca lowered herself onto the beach and smiled at the dog. "I see you've made a new friend."

"He came up to me."

Aunt Rebecca glanced over at her, her dark eyes wide and unflinching. "Dogs can sense when people are upset, you know."

Lily swallowed past the dryness in her throat. "I didn't know that."

Rebecca stretched her legs out and placed her arms

out on either side of her. "Do you want to talk about it? You don't have to if you don't want to."

Lily released a deep, shaky breath. "I want to. I just don't know how much good it will do." A heartbeat later, she turned to her aunt and studied her weathered, angular face in the midmorning sun. "My dad called."

Rebecca's expression turned grim. "I take it he isn't happy you're here?"

Lily sighed. "That's an understatement. He started lecturing me and making it seem like it was my fault."

Rebecca placed a hand on top of Lily's, her expression turning soft. "I'm sorry."

Lily's eyes filled with tears. "He made me believe she didn't want me. My whole life, he acted like I was this big disappointment, like I could never do anything right, and I always thought it was because he blamed me for Kelly leaving."

Lily had been led to believe that if it weren't for her, Kelly would've stayed.

Her father had never let her forget it.

Or so she thought.

Rebecca draped an arm over her shoulders. "You're not a disappointment, and you're not the reason Kelly left. Your mother left because of him, because she wanted a different kind of life than the one she had. There is so much more to the story, honey. She had to leave."

Lily brought her head to rest against her aunt's shoulder. "I don't even know why he lied to me all those years. He could've told me the truth instead of letting me hate her. Instead, he let me waste all that time..."

Aunt Rebecca exhaled. "Look, I don't know why your father did what he did. None of us do. We all spent years wondering, but I do know one thing. Your mother would be happy you found your way back here, even if it did take you forty-nine years."

Lily choked back a laugh. "I did take a few detours along the way."

Rebecca patted her hand. "The important thing is that you're here. That's all that matters. All of the rest... We'll figure it out together."

Lily drew back to look at her aunt. "How can you be so calm about it? You should be furious."

"I am," Rebecca replied without looking at her. Lily watched as her aunt studied the waters, a thoughtful expression on her face as her eyes grew misty and her smile turned wistful. "But it's not going to do you any good, will it?"

Silence stretched between them.

"Aunt Rebecca, I want to ask you something, but I don't want to upset you."

Rebecca turned so she was facing Lily completely. "You want to know about Sean?"

"How were you able to get through it? Watching your husband get sick and not being able to do anything about it?"

"When Sean was first diagnosed, I was obsessed. I used to stay up most nights doing research and talking to doctors. I tried to do everything in order to help him beat it, but it didn't help. When they told us he was out of time, it was Sean who knocked some sense into me."

"How?"

"He didn't want me to spend our remaining time trying to fix something that couldn't be fixed. Instead, he wanted us to make the most of the time we had left together." Rebecca touched the ring on her middle finger, her voice catching toward the end. "I've tried to carry that advice with me ever since. I know it was harder on Angie; the two of them were really close... At least she talks to me about it; your other cousins, Rob and Terry, won't even mention him."

Lily took her aunt's hand and squeezed. "I'm sorry. I can't even imagine what that must've been like for you."

"Loss is a part of life, Lily. We might not like it, and we might try to fight against it, but it's inevitable. The only thing we can do is make room for it and learn to live with it so it's not as heavy to carry."

Lily glanced away and swallowed.

The golden retriever barked, bringing them both back to the present with a jolt. Rebecca rose to her feet to pat him. Lily dusted herself off and did the same. In silence, they walked along the edge of the water together.

Lily knew she was where she was supposed to be. She was done bowing down to her father.

Chapter Six

Lily sent Aunt Heather a text and tapped her feet while she waited. She reviewed the grocery list on her phone and smiled when her aunt sent a reply back. Then, Lily reached for her purse, adjusted the strap on her shoulder, and exited out the front door of the beach house.

Outside, it was a warm Sunday afternoon, and Lily walked to the supermarket.

There, she picked up a selection of cheeses, cold cuts, and olives. After wandering through the well-stocked aisles, listening to country music in the background, she stopped at their wine selection. She skimmed through some of the labels and decided on three bottles of Pinot Grigio. At the checkout counter, Lily couldn't stop smiling to herself.

Being in Provincetown and getting to know her mother's family had that effect on her. Over the past few days, she'd been getting to know everyone and familiarizing herself with her surroundings in the hopes the town was what she needed. Little by little, it was healing the scars she carried and opening her up to new possibilities.

Not to mention providing inspiration for her book.

Being out by the water and surrounded by people who were living active and healthy lives was a great source of inspiration. It provided plenty of ideas for her book, a guide on how to eat delicious and healthy food.

With a smile, Lily stepped out of the store and back onto the sunlit street. During the walk back, she kept taking her phone out to glance at her screen.

She tried not to be uneasy about the fact she hadn't heard from her father since their phone call. Considering how proud Eric Taylor was, she doubted she was going to be hearing from him for a while. Already, she pictured him spinning a story about how her mother's family had poisoned her against him and driven a wedge between them.

Before she knew it, Lily was back in front of the beach house and carrying her groceries inside. She arranged everything on the charcuterie board, poured herself a glass of Pinot Grigio, and carried it outside. In the doorway, she paused to grab a handful of Aunt Heather's letters and took them outside with her. Lily fingered another envelope slowly, deftly, as if it were the most delicate thing in the world. Then, she held it up to the light and began to read.

Dear Lily,

I heard you're engaged, and I've looked him up. He looks charming and handsome, but I wonder if he's the right fit for you. I hope he makes you happy. Seeing you in the tabloids, with his arm draped around you like that, reminds me of when your mother met Eric.

She was so happy then.

He promised her the world and everything in it, and she believed him. I wished I had told her the truth then about how I got an uneasy feeling whenever I was around him. Of course, I didn't know any better. I thought Eric was just protective. I had no idea he was going to try and isolate your mother after marriage, and I definitely didn't know he was going to destroy her self-esteem.

I remember the summer your father's family came to vacation here. I disliked your father the minute I set eyes on him, but Kelly wouldn't listen. She was so headstrong back then and so stubborn. She thought she knew better than all of us. I think I was the only one who wasn't surprised when the two of them ran off together.

It broke our parents' hearts when she left like that.

I should've known when she got pregnant right away that something was wrong. Kelly always said she would wait to have children, and once your father's career took off... Everything went downhill from there. Honestly, I'm not even sure why I'm telling you all of this except that I hope your fate doesn't turn out to be the same. I hope your future husband doesn't make you feel like a hostage in your own home and make you feel small in every way possible.

I didn't tell Kelly the truth, and it was my responsibility, as her older sister, to look out for her. I don't want to make the same mistake with you, Lily. You're my niece, and I've never met you, but I already feel protective over you. I hope you're happy, and please know you can come to me at any time.

. . .

With love,
    Aunt Heather

When Lily lowered the letter and saw her aunt Heather standing at the top steps of the veranda, her hand flew to her chest. She stood up, set the letter down, and unlocked the door leading inside. Heather's eyes moved to the stack of letters and then back to Lily's face. Wordlessly, she pulled her in for a hug, and Lily shuddered.

A swell of emotion—heartache, frustration, and pain—grew in her chest.

"I had no idea it was so bad," Lily murmured after she sat down. She pushed the board closer to Heather and sighed. "I wish I had known all of this."

"Sweetheart, you were a baby," Heather replied. "None of this was your fault, and you couldn't have done anything."

"Was he really holding her hostage in her own house?"

Heather's expression tightened. "He was. I'm sorry, Lily. I know he's your father, but I think you're old enough to know the truth. When Eric's career took off, his relationship with your mother went downhill, and it never recovered."

Lily set her wine glass down and sucked in a harsh breath. "Was he... Did he hurt her?"

Heather cleared her throat. "Mostly verbally, sometimes physically, but rarely. He used to constantly criticize everything about her. Eventually, he started cheating on her, and that's when he isolated her. He made her feel like she couldn't leave."

Lily's throat turned dry. "What did she do?"

"She was still able to talk to me," Heather whispered, a myriad of emotions dancing across her face; her expression changed and darkened with each one, from yearning and sadness to frustration and finally resignation. "I tried to convince her to leave him, but she wouldn't at first. Then she began to wonder what would happen to you. Your father is a powerful man. He wouldn't have just let her take you."

Lily sat back against the chair and gripped the armrest, needing it to keep herself upright and steady. "Is that why she left?"

"We made a plan for her to leave, and Eric found out. He threatened to have her committed if she ever tried to take you away. I promised your mother I would find a way to keep an eye on you, but I knew if I didn't get her out then, she wasn't going to make it out alive."

A pregnant pause followed, during which Lily's blood roared in her ears.

She couldn't imagine how difficult it must've been for her mother to have to choose between her daughter and getting out of there alive. While Lily herself was sure she wouldn't have been able to leave her own kids behind, she couldn't say for certain. Lily had, after all, barely survived her own similarly abusive marriage. Her mother had done the best she could under the circumstances.

Heather set her wine glass down and leaned forward. She took both of Lily's hands in hers and held her gaze. "I know this is difficult to hear. I don't want to make this any harder. I just wanted you to know that your mother did fight for you. When she got to Falmouth, all she could think about, all she could do, was try to find a way to get you out."

Lily pressed her lips together and nodded.

Heather squeezed her hand again. "Why don't we talk about this some more later? I actually came back to give you some good news."

Lily cleared her throat. "More good news? How did I get so lucky?"

Heather chuckled and released her hands. She tightened the shawl around her shoulders and looked out at the water. "I've got a friend of mine who owns a wellness spa, Sabrina Heard. She's been looking for a dietician to rent out a space there. I might have mentioned your name."

Lily smiled. "Aunt Heather, you've already done so much for me."

Heather waved her comment away. "Don't be silly. You're my niece. I'm happy to help."

Lily stretched her legs out in front of her and sighed. "I don't know. I hadn't really thought about going back to work... I have that book I told you I was working on."

Heather nodded. "Well, there's no harm in checking out the space and seeing how you feel. Even if you do it part time, I'm sure you and Sabrina can come to some sort of agreement."

"All right. I'll talk to her, but I can't promise anything."

Heather picked her glass up and touched it to Lily's. "No promises, deal. I just think it would be a good opportunity for you to get out more, meet more people, that sort of thing."

Lily eyed her aunt over the rim of the glass. "Thank you."

With the settlement from Lance following their divorce and the next several chapters of her book already outlined, Lily doubted she wanted to commit to anything else. Having spent years dedicating most of her time to her children or maintaining their social image, Lily wasn't even sure she had it in her to return to the field in a more stable capacity.

Working part time with a few clients here and there had suited her just fine. It still did.

But she appreciated her aunt going to all that effort and didn't want to disappoint her. Taking a look around the place and having a chat with her aunt's friend couldn't hurt anyway.

With a smile in her aunt's direction, Lily set her glass down, and they continued to make easy conversation.

A short while later, the doorbell rang, and Aunt Heather's daughter, Tammy, emerged. She gave her mom a quick hug before pulling up her own chair. "Why didn't you tell me we were having a party? I would've brought something."

Heather made a vague hand gesture. "Lily's already made more than enough food."

Lily threw her head back and laughed. "I've seen how much food you guys make. This is nothing in comparison."

Tammy reached for an olive and popped it into her mouth. "This is really delicious."

Aunt Heather draped an arm over her daughter's shoulders and kissed the side of her head. "How was your day at work today? Your dad keeping you on your toes?"

Tammy smiled and relaxed. "Yeah, you know how Dad is. He and Luke are always butting heads though. It's exhausting having to be their referee."

"No one does it as well as you," Aunt Heather replied, smiling in her daughter's direction. "Did you know your cousin is a dietician?"

Tammy poured herself some wine. "Yeah, I heard. I've never met a dietician before, Lily. That must be cool."

Lily nodded and reached for the blanket behind her. She tucked it around her legs and smiled. "I don't even remember how I got into it, but my youngest, Lauren, is studying to become a dietician too, so I must've done something right."

"You must be so proud."

Lily poured herself some more wine and eyed her cousin, taking in the high, arched brows, almond-shaped eyes, and a row of perfect white teeth. "You've got two kids, right? I think I met them the other night."

"Tania and Abby. Tania graduated a year ago and is trying out different things, and Abby can't seem to settle on a job either. It keeps me up at night, but I mean, that's part of the job, right?"

Aunt Heather snorted. "There's also the fact your husband is a firefighter. I don't know how you go to sleep every night knowing he's out there, putting his life on the line."

Tammy's lips lifted into a half smile. "James has been doing this for years, Mom. He can handle himself."

Aunt Heather muttered something under her breath, and the three of them erupted into laughter.

Lily couldn't remember the last time she'd had this much fun.

She was suddenly immensely grateful for the circumstances that brought her here, her mother's letters that made her feel closer to her, and the family who had always loved her.

With her mother's family by her side, the future didn't seem so terrifying.

Chapter Seven

Lily set down her menu and looked around at her aunts and their daughters, all gathered around a table in the back at the Herring Cove Café. "That sounds like way too much food. Are we expecting anyone else?"

Everyone burst into laughter, and her aunts gave her identical indulgent smiles.

Aunt Heather patted her hand and set her own menu down. "Trust me, you're going to love every single dish."

Lily leaned backward in her seat and glanced around, taking in the blue-and-white walls, the wooden tables scattered throughout, and the waitstaff moving at a steady but relaxed rhythm, all of them dressed in blue-and-beige uniforms. Now and again, when they came up to the table, Aunt Rebecca and Aunt Heather introduced her with smiles and broad hand gestures.

It felt a little like being caught in the headlights, but Lily tried not to mind. Since they had already missed out on so much of her life, she knew her aunts were trying to make up for everything.

When Lily straightened her back and sat up, she looked over at her cousins, seated next to each other, all of them wearing varying shades of the same dress.

Without looking up from her menu, Terry spoke, "Ang, aren't you worried that the kitchen is going to fall apart without you?"

Angie narrowed her eyes in Terry's direction and scowled. "You're just annoyed because of Lara. But you seem to be forgetting, when I hired her last year, she ignored all of the customers and got their orders wrong."

Terry huffed. "That's because you gave her too much to handle. She's only nineteen."

"We were both holding down jobs when we were her age, and don't even get me started on Glen Jr. Does he even know how to have a full conversation without grunting or referencing something on TikTok?"

Tammy leaned over the table and caught Lily's gaze. "The two of them could be like this for a while. I wouldn't worry though."

Lily reached for her glass of water. "Yeah, my daughters are the same. They've gotten better with age, but they used to be so difficult when they were younger."

Angie turned her gaze to Lily. "How old are your daughters now?"

"Sara is twenty-two. She's getting a bachelor's degree in science at NYU. She's dating this econ major...Jake Baker... I'm trying to be supportive, but he doesn't make it easy."

A waitress emerged, setting a few dishes of food in front of them, including lobster rolls, fried clams, and scallops.

Lily's stomach grumbled at the sight.

Tammy gave her a sympathetic smile. "Abby is dating

someone I don't like either. He rides a motorcycle and has several tattoos."

Lily frowned. "Sounds like he and Jake would get along."

Tammy burst into laughter. "Oh, I hope not. What about your other daughter, Lauren? She's the one you told me about the other day, right? The one who's studying to become a dietician?"

Lily took another sip of her drink. "Lauren's got laser-sharp focus. When she sets her mind to something, she doesn't quit."

It was both sweet and a little unnerving how much Lauren reminded Lily of herself. While she admired her daughter's persistence and hoped it paid off in the long run, the last thing she wanted was for Lauren to end up like her.

Learning what her dad had been doing behind the scenes, pulling the strings and manipulating everything in her life, didn't sit well with her. Not even the suspicion Eric had done it out of a misguided attempt to protect her made things better. If anything, it made things worse.

She would hate to imagine Lance doing the same to their daughter.

With a frown, Lily set her drink down and fixed her gaze on Tammy. "So, what's it like working at a real estate company here? It's a beautiful town. I'm sure a lot of people like buying beach houses and stuff."

Tammy reached for her own drink and took a long sip. "We do pretty well, most of the time. My dad's been in the business for a while, so he taught me everything I know, but there are times when things get a little...hard to handle."

Angie snorted. "That's putting it mildly. Tammy has a habit of being a little too trusting."

Tammy set her drink down with a little more force than necessary, causing some of the liquid to slosh over. "That's not true. Besides, it's better to try with people than to close yourself off."

Terry rolled her eyes. "You two need to let that go already. You're never going to see eye to eye on this."

Lily glanced between the three of them and cleared her throat. "So, Terry, do you enjoy being a criminal lawyer?"

Her cousin was nothing at all like her ex-husband, a criminal lawyer, who was always eagle-eyed and cataloging everything. Lily had almost forgotten a lot of criminal lawyers were normal people with real lives, not people who spent most of their time digging up dirt and finding ways to back people into corners.

Her ex, like her father, wasn't much different in that regard.

Terry shrugged. "I like what I do most of the time, but sometimes, I think maybe I'm in the wrong business."

Angie patted her sister's hand. "That's an understatement. Terry used to bring a lot of cases home in the beginning, and she'd be crying."

"You've got to have really thick skin to make it in this business."

"And good connections," Angie added between bites of food. "But you know all about that, right, Lily? Aunt Heather mentioned your dad is a lawyer."

Lily's stomach twisted into knots. "So is my ex."

Aunt Rebecca picked up her glass and cleared her throat. "So, Lily, what do you think of the café so far? I know it doesn't look like much, but our staff is great."

Lily shot her aunt a grateful look and cast another glance around, admiring the way tiny particles of light danced off every surface. "I like how it's set up. It's small, but it's cozy."

"It's exactly what we were going for," Aunt Heather replied, pausing to dab at her mouth with a napkin. "Our parents spent a lot of time scoping out places before settling on this one. It's a great location because it's in the middle of town, but we're also within walking distance of a lot of vendors, et cetera."

Lily scooped a handful of fried clams, drizzled in lemon and mayonnaise, onto her plate. "The food is really fresh."

Aunt Heather beamed. "It's brought in every morning. I've gone out a few times. There's nothing like being awake at that time of day and being out near the water. It's very calming."

Lily flashed her aunt another smile and bit into her food.

It was the most delicious thing she'd ever tried, the thick and creamy mixture complementing each other well and causing a burst of rich flavor in her mouth.

While Lily tried a little bit of everything on the table, she paused at the clam chowder in particular, marveling at the hearty, flavored soup made of clams, potatoes, and onion. The creamy and chunky concoction lingered on her tongue while her aunts spoke, going into great detail about the layout of the café and offering her some back-story to the staff.

Connected in one way or another to their family, everyone had a triumphant story that led to them being employed there. Lily wasn't sure if she was impressed or intimidated by the fact her aunts knew so much and actually cared about the well-being of their employees beyond their nine-to-five jobs. She'd never seen anything like it before.

It made the café even more welcoming and wholesome.

"Aunt Rebecca, I'm not sure how you manage to stay on top of things like this, but you're doing a great job," Lily told her with a smile. "I definitely couldn't be in charge of an entire inn and its staff and do half as well as you."

Aunt Rebecca waved her comment away. "It takes some time, patience, and a lot of practice."

"And late nights being locked in the kitchen in her underwear," Aunt Heather whispered next to her.

Lily coughed and choked on her drink.

Aunt Heather thumped Lily on the back, the easy smile never leaving her face. Once Lily's vision cleared, she wiped her mouth and sat up straighter.

She glanced over at her aunt Heather, who gave her a mischievous wink and returned to her food. Lily looked back at her cousins, all of whom were engaged in small talk and easy chatter.

"Lara and Glen Jr. seem great, by the way," Lily offered, her gaze settling on Terry. "I'm not sure how you managed to juggle being a lawyer and being a mom, but I think it's great."

Terry set down her fork and reached for her drink. "Glen did a lot of the heavy lifting in the beginning. I honestly couldn't have managed those first few years, especially when my career was taking off."

Lily gave Terry a sympathetic smile. "I'm sorry about your husband."

Terry hid her expression behind her glass. "Thank you."

Angie cleared her throat. "Aunt Heather, you and I both know you're watching your weight the same way you used to watch your patients. With a lot of heart and a lot of discipline. You can stop hiding crumbs under the table."

Aunt Heather chuckled. "How else do you think I stayed at the top of my game as a nurse?"

Terry shook her head. "You're a force to be reckoned with, Auntie. We all know that already."

"We're so happy to have you here, Lily," Aunt Heather said a little too loudly. "You have no idea how long we've waited for this. But better late than never, right?"

Lily nodded and touched her glass to her aunt's. "Hear, hear."

After another round of cheers, Lily glanced around the table with tears in her eyes, overwhelmed by the outpouring of love and gratitude she was feeling.

Already, she could picture herself doing this sort of thing regularly.

It made her feel dizzy and lightheaded, like she could float right off the ground.

Lily wiped her mouth and pushed her chair back. "Where's the bathroom?"

Aunt Rebecca pointed to a hallway in the back. "Down there and to the right. You can't miss it."

Conversation rose and fell around Lily as she walked away, a comfortable sensation blossoming in the center of her stomach. In the bathroom, she noticed her flushed cheeks and the twinkle in her eyes, making her smile. After patting her hands dry, she cast one last look in the mirror and stepped out, colliding face-first with a tall, broad-shouldered man with the kindest hazel eyes she'd ever seen.

"Easy there. You all right?"

Lily righted herself and took an involuntary step back. "I am so sorry. I think I've definitely had too much food."

His lips twitched in amusement. "That's definitely an excuse I haven't heard before. Do you remember how to get back to your table?"

"That's the round thing with chairs around it."

He burst into laughter, and some of the lines around his eyes eased. "Yeah, you definitely know where you're going. Come on, I'm headed back that way anyway."

Lily peered at him. "I can manage, you know. It's only a food high, after all."

"That's the best kind of high." He glanced back at her, and she caught a brief glimpse of his tanned face and strong nose with a slight dent in the middle. "First time at the restaurant?"

"That obvious?"

Together, they poured out of the hallway and back into the main part of the restaurant, where her family's laughter reached them. Her aunts waved them over, and her mysterious stranger didn't bat an eye or miss a step. Instead, he walked her back to the table and paused to give them all a wave and a smile.

"I see you've met the inn's caretaker. Lily, this is Ben Vasquez. In addition to taking care of the inn, he also handles all of the excursions for the guests, so if you want anything to do with fishing, sailing, or any of those things, he's your guy."

Ben held his hand out. "Nice to meet you, Lily."

Lily slipped her hand into his and was surprised to feel a jolt of electricity course through her. "You too."

"Lily is our niece," Aunt Rebecca added after a brief pause. "She's visiting from New York City."

Ben nodded and withdrew his hand. "Welcome to Provincetown, Lily. We hope you like it here."

Lily looked away, a flush rising up her neck and her cheeks. "Thanks. I think I will."

When Ben walked away a short while later, Lily tried not to stare after him and ended up shushing her cousins and ignoring their teasing. For the rest of their lunch, Lily sat there, basking in the warm glow of their presence and wondering how she had gotten so lucky.

Chapter Eight

"I just think you should take it easy, sweetheart." Lily used the back of her hand to wipe the steam away from the mirror. Then she set her phone down on the sink and picked up her comb. "You're taking on a lot."

"You always say that, Mom."

Sara sounded winded and out of breath, but she usually did whenever Lily talked to her in the morning. Like her mom, Sara took staying in shape very seriously and never missed a chance to go on her morning run, much to the dismay of her boyfriend, Jake, who preferred to spend his mornings on the couch in front of the TV.

"Maybe try listening to your mother, then," Lily said in between mouthfuls of toothpaste. "Sometimes, I know what I'm talking about."

Sara blew out a breath. "You always know what you're talking about, Mom. I just want to remind you that people take on a lot more than me."

Lily spat out a mouthful of toothpaste and frowned. "You're already taking on a full course load for the semester and working part time. And didn't you mention wanting to intern over the summer?"

Sara laughed, and Lily heard chatter in the background. "Mom, I can handle it. Besides, you know how competitive the job market is these days. If I want a leg up, I have to have an impressive résumé."

"I think it's plenty impressive already," Lily offered, pausing to set down her comb. "I'm sure Jake would agree with me."

While the two of them didn't agree on much, when it came to Sara's well-being and her tendency to push herself too hard, Lily and Jake were in complete agreement. Trying to find some common ground with her daughter's boyfriend was hard, but most days, she succeeded in reminding herself that he was Sara's choice.

It was all that mattered.

And he did care about her daughter, in his own kind of way.

"Jake is being really supportive, actually," Sara replied after a brief pause. "He's even started learning how to separate colored laundry from the whites."

Lily smiled and took a step back. "I'm glad, sweetheart. Just remember to take it easy. You're already on track to becoming a great biologist."

"Thanks, Mom. I know you're trying really hard not to lecture me right now, unlike Dad, so I really appreciate that."

Lily stepped back into the main room and flung her closet door open. "You've spoken about this?"

Sara sighed. "You know what things are like with Dad. He doesn't really listen. He just kind of talks at you."

Lily set down a pair of shorts and a sleeveless top. "He means well."

"I still can't believe you're defending him," Sara muttered darkly. "You know you're allowed to be upset and call him names."

"He's still your dad."

And regardless of her own personal feelings about the matter, Lily wasn't going to let them cloud their perception of him. All of her kids were old enough to form their own opinions about Lance without her trying to influence them. Besides, she didn't think poisoning them against Lance would do any of them any good, not when they were all trying to move on from the divorce and heal.

"You're a much better person than I am," Sara told her, a smile in her voice. "Anyway, I've got to go. I've got a shift before my noon class. Talk to you later?"

"Talk to you later. Love you."

"Love you too, Mom."

As soon as Lily pulled on her shorts and top, her phone rang, and Lauren's name flashed across the screen. She smiled and cradled the phone between her neck and shoulders.

"Hi, Mom. I just thought I'd check in before class. I didn't wake you, did I?"

Lily chuckled. "No, sweetheart. You know I like to be up early to go on my morning run."

"Yeah, but I thought you'd take the chance to learn to develop different habits while you're there, you know, be a little lazy. You've earned it."

Lily gathered her hair into a high ponytail and stepped out of her room and into the hallway. She took the stairs two at a time, pausing at the picture of her mom at the bottom of the stairs. With a smile, she touched two fingers to the glass and felt the familiar tug in the center of her chest. Lauren said something into her ear, and Lily gave a slight shake of her head and took the last of the stairs.

"Sorry, honey, what was that?"

"I asked how it's going with everyone. You sound happy."

Lily stepped into the kitchen and grabbed a banana off the counter. "I am. Provincetown is nothing at all like New York. I like how calm and relaxed everyone is. I think you'd really like it."

"No offense, Mom, but it sounds like I'd be bored. You know I like to be challenged."

Lily tore off a piece of her banana. "It's okay to slow down too, sweetheart. You sound just like your sister. You two need to take it easy." After snatching her keys off the counter, Lily stepped out onto the front porch and paused to tie her shoes. "Have you gotten the hang of things yet? Which professors did you get?"

"Don't tell me you're going to start micromanaging now," Lauren teased, her voice drifting in and out of focus. "I thought we agreed I wasn't going to tell you who I got, so you didn't influence my opinion of them."

Lily stood up straighter and turned her key in the lock. "We didn't agree on that, did we?"

Lauren chuckled. "Yeah, we did."

Lily took the stairs two at a time and hugged the side of the house, moving with the wraparound veranda until she reached the back. Carefully, she made her way down the dune, pausing to gawk at the panoramic view of the water.

She didn't think she could ever get used to it or the way it glistened and sparkled underneath the early morning sun, set against a backdrop of clear blue skies. It wasn't long before the slope opened onto the walking path, the same one she'd taken over the past few days.

It had become a routine for her, one she enjoyed every single morning.

"Mom, I've got to go. I want to get to class early and find a good seat. I'll call you after, okay? Have a good run."

"Thank you, sweetheart. Have a good class."

When the line went dead, Lily tucked her phone into her pocket and raised her arms up on either side of her. She kept up a steady pace as she descended onto the beach, kicking up sand and dirt as she did. With no one else on the beach, it felt like she was the only person in Provincetown.

She couldn't help but compare it to the hustle and grind of New York. In the entire time she'd lived there, Lily didn't think she'd ever once gone for a run alone or even been surrounded by such peace and quiet that she could hear her own soft, muted breathing.

It almost made her miss the hot dog guy, blocks away from their apartment, and the woman who owned a newspaper booth across from him.

Lily cocked her head to the side and could almost hear the familiar sounds of their bickering, barely distinguishable against the screeching of tires and dogs howling in the distance.

With a sigh, Lily made her way back to the house an hour later and hurried into the shower. When she came out, a thin mist following her into the room, she stopped in front of her closet. Suddenly, she saw herself as she used to be in their old apartment, with her hair already done, a pressed suit laid out, and a few touches of makeup on her face.

By now, Lily would've already had her entire day mapped out.

It was exciting to realize, other than a quick meeting with her aunt's friend, Lily had nothing else planned.

She hummed to herself as she tossed her running clothes into the hamper and pulled on a knee-length skirt and button-down blouse. Lily left her hair in loose waves around her shoulders and snatched her purse off the dresser.

A short while later, she came to a stop outside the Herring Wellness Center and Spa, a three-story brick building with a cream exterior, white shutters, a single chimney adorning the roofline, and a wraparound veranda that disappeared behind the back of the building. She fished her phone out of her purse, held it up to her ear, and waited. Before she could even dial the number, a petite woman dressed in a jumpsuit with honey-blond hair and expressive green eyes waved at her.

"Hi, you must be Lily." Sabrina Heard held her hand out, her eyes sparkling with mischief and humor. "Your aunts have told me a lot about you."

"They've told me a lot about you too. Thank you for doing this," Lily replied, pausing to give her a firm shake. "This looks really impressive."

"Wait till you see inside."

Sabrina gave her a quick wink and stepped to the side. She pushed the door open and motioned to Lily. With a smile, Lily moved past the chairs set up out front and stepped in, noticing the hardwood floors, high, arched ceilings, and sunlight pouring in through every inch of the reception area. A set of winding stairs led to the floor above, and the smell of incense and oils hung in the air.

Lily crept forward, matching her pace to Sabrina's, who made a beeline for the front desk, where a man and a woman sat, dressed identically in blue-and-white uniforms.

Sabrina held her arms out on either side of her. "Welcome to the Herring Wellness Center and Spa. We're open every day of the week except for Saturdays, and we offer a wide variety of options for our guests."

Sabrina paused to hand Lily a menu, and she skimmed it quickly, impressed at the number of services they offered, from full body waxing to couple's massages and everything in between. When she was done, she handed Sabrina the menu back with a smile. Sabrina motioned to her and led her through the sliding French doors, which opened up into a large, empty stretch of land with grass underneath her feet, trees lined up on either side, and a wraparound fence offering an unobstructed view of the water.

Lily slowed her pace. "I know you must get tired of this, but the view..."

Sabrina smiled. "I don't think I could ever get tired of it. I'm not sure how much your aunt told you about the place, but we offer indoor and outdoor meditation classes as well as indoor and outdoor yoga. Our guests have the option to join classes or practice separately."

Lily paused in the middle and spun around to look up at the center of the building, picturesque and scenic from where she stood. "I understand you also have a sauna with a steam room and indoor pool."

"We also offer Moroccan baths, and we've got an in-house masseuse and physical therapist."

Lily let out a low whistle. "Honestly, this is already pretty impressive. I'm not sure I'd be of any use to you here. I'm sure my aunt already told you I haven't been a full-time dietician in a while. I've had some part-time clients here and there, but I've been focusing on...other things."

Sabrina nodded. "That's fine. I don't see that being an issue."

Lily shifted from one foot to the other and glanced over at Sabrina, who looked serene and proud as she regarded the center. "I'm working on a book right now. It's about clean eating, superfoods, cleanses—those types of things. I'm not sure how that'll fit into all of this."

Sabrina twisted to face her, a smile hovering on the edge of her lips. "If you'd like to offer programs part time, I'm sure we could find an arrangement that works too."

Lily raised her eyebrow. "Wouldn't you need me to be in the office? Or at least on-site as part of the staff?"

Sabrina laughed and shook her head. "No, we're pretty flexible here. I like to make sure my staff is committed but also given some leeway. I think it makes for a healthy work environment."

Lily nodded. "I agree."

But she hadn't thought of working any jobs, part time or otherwise.

If it weren't for her aunt Heather, Lily wasn't even sure she'd be here, but she hadn't wanted her aunt's good work to go to waste, nor did she want to leave a bad impression. Sabrina Heard was, after all, not only the owner and manager of the wellness center and spa but also one of her aunt's closest friends. Blowing her off hadn't seemed like the right choice. And Lily was glad she was getting a closer look at the grounds and the layout of the place.

"Why don't you think about it and let me know? There's no rush anyway."

Lily stood up straighter and smiled. "I'd like that. Thank you. So, you and my aunt have known each other for a while, huh?"

Sabrina's eyes crinkled around the corners. "The stories I could tell you."

"I've got some time."

Sabrina threw her head back and laughed. "I like you already. Why don't we go into my office, and I can tell you all about the time your aunt nearly burned the inn down?"

Lily chuckled. "Lead the way."

Chapter Nine

Lily lifted a hand up to her face and squinted into the sun-soaked distance. "You guys made it. Welcome."

Lily ended the call as the black sedan came to a stop next to the curb. Her stepsister, Sophia, came out first, sunglasses perched on top of her head and a large bag slung over her shoulder. When the car came to a complete stop, her stepbrother, Ian, slipped out next, phone pressed to his ear and a harried look on his face. In a few strides, they were both in front of her, wheeling their bags behind them.

Lily drew Sophia in for a hug and lingered. "How was the drive up?"

"It was great. Sorry, we're a little late. Someone had to keep stopping to use the bathroom."

Ian ended the call and gave Lily a quick hug. "I drink a lot of coffee."

"And you eat a lot of donuts." Sophia patted his stomach affectionately. "Could you be any more of a stereotype?"

Ian sniffed. "Not all cops like donuts, you know. Some like bagels."

Lily chuckled and pushed the door open. "Whatever keeps you guys alert and ready works for me. As far as I'm concerned, you can have all the donuts and bagels."

Sophia snorted on her way past. "Lily is being too nice. I'm not going to go easy on you."

Ian left their bags by the door and wandered into the living room, pausing to peer out the sliding back door. "You've never gone easy on me anyway. Lily, I love your view. This place is amazing."

"Yeah, we were talking about it on the car ride over. We've been invited a few times, but we've never been able to come and spend time here."

Ian spun around to face them and shoved both hands into the pockets of his jeans. "It feels weird to be here without Mom."

Silence stretched between them.

Lily cleared her throat and ignored the nervous flutter in her stomach. "How's Lucy?"

"She's got this big wedding she's planning. I think she's actually glad to have me out of the house for a bit," Ian replied with a shake of his head. "Sometimes, I feel like she can't wait for moments when she gets the house to herself."

Lily smiled. "With three kids, things can get hectic."

Ian nodded. "Kelli and Dana manage well enough. It's Dean I worry about. He comes over so often I feel like he practically still lives there."

Sophia stepped into the kitchen and rummaged through the fridge. She pulled out a few containers and a bottle of wine. "He practically does. Doesn't he still have some of his stuff in the basement, and doesn't he do the laundry there?"

Ian rolled his eyes. "It's because the washing machine in their building is always busted, and the room he's renting is pretty small."

Sophia carried a few more containers and kicked the refrigerator door shut with the back of her leg. "I feel like he's just going to end up renting out your basement. Wouldn't it be easier that way?"

"Don't give him any ideas, please," Ian said with a shake of his head. "Lucy is already annoyed I'm giving him so much leeway."

Sophia opened and closed several cupboards, setting out plates and cups as she did. "You should be thankful they're around. I barely even see Zac. He's doing this humanitarian habitat program. I'm really proud of him, but I do miss him."

Lily moved to the other side of the counter and surveyed the stuff there. "Why don't I give you a hand? Where's Zac right now?"

Sophia pried a box open and took out some cheese. "Somewhere in Africa. I don't even remember where, and now Zoe is talking about joining him. I'm trying to convince her to do an internship first."

With a smile, the three of them carried the tray of sandwiches and wine bottle and stepped out onto the back veranda. After arranging the food and wine glasses, the three of them pulled up their chairs and sat them down next to each other. When the afternoon sun was high in the sky, the three of them were clutching their sides and laughing while telling stories.

On the third glass of wine, Lily suggested a walk along the beach.

Ian and Sophia fell into step beside her, a warm breeze drifting past them. When they reached the bottom of the stairs, the three of them fell quiet, walking barefoot along the sand. A flock of birds shot up into the sky, and Lily paused to watch them.

"So, is it hard to co-parent with your ex?"

Lily lowered her head and looked directly at Sophia. "It takes some work, I guess, but we're managing."

Sophia frowned. "It sounds like he's not making it easy."

"Lance isn't the kind of person who's used to being told no," Lily revealed with a shake of her head. She paused along the edge of the water and blew out a breath. "But I'm trying my best for the kids."

Keeping the peace wasn't easy, not with Lance criticizing her every move, but she didn't want the alternative. As far as she was concerned, Lance was, and always would be, the father of her children, and she was going to do her best to preserve that.

Even when all she wanted to do was give him a piece of her mind.

Sophia stood on her left and ran a hand over her face. "I know what that's like. When Darren and I first got divorced, it was hard. It took us a while to find a rhythm. Eventually, I think realizing we don't have to be on opposite sides of this helped."

Lily snuck a glance at Sophia, who had a far-off, dazed expression on her face, like she was reliving something private. "You sound like you're handling it well."

Sophia sighed. "Most days, we manage. Other days, it's hard. Hopefully, things work out between you and Lance either way. You mentioned having two other siblings?"

Lily nodded and looked out at the water. "Lucas and Sylvie. Lucas works with our dad at his firm, and Sylvie is a real estate agent at Sotheby's."

Ian came to a stop next to her. "I'm sorry things are difficult with your ex."

Lily twisted her head to look at him. "Thank you. I'm really glad you guys came out here. Are you sure you can't stay longer?"

Sophia draped an arm over her shoulders. "We'll be coming up so often, you'll get sick of it."

"Yeah, you better get used to us, sis," Ian teased, pausing to stretch his arms up over his head. "I can see why Mom used to love it here."

Lily swallowed past the lump in her throat. "How—how did she die?"

Sophia and Ian exchanged a quick look. Sophia squeezed her shoulders and straightened her back. "It was a robbery gone bad."

Lily's heart was pounding in her ears. "Aunt Heather only told me bits and pieces. I think it's too painful for her."

Ian nodded, and a shadow settled over his face. "It's painful for everyone to talk about. We were only a year old when it happened, so we don't remember anything. Dad was on patrol that night, and he's the one who got the call."

A lump rose in the back of Lily's throat, and a hard knot settled in the pit of her stomach.

She couldn't imagine receiving a phone call like that, the kind that turned her whole world upside down.

"He doesn't talk about what it was like to get there and not be allowed in to see her," Sophia continued in a quiet voice. "But we know it was hard for him."

"Why does he think it was a robbery gone wrong?"

Ian picked up a pebble and tossed it into the water. "He said the whole place was turned upside down, like they were looking for something, but they didn't actually take much."

Lily cleared her throat. "So, Ke—Mom was just there at the wrong time?"

Sophia removed her arm from around Lily's shoulders. "We try not to think about her like that. We have very few memories of her, but our dad told us she never stopped talking about you. She tried really hard to be reunited with you, Lily."

Lily brought her head to rest against Sophia's shoulders. "I'm glad we can all talk about her."

Because the more she learned about her mother, the more she realized Kelly Wilson had done her best. She had fallen in love with the wrong man, been forced to get herself out in order to survive, and had spent her remaining two years on Earth fighting to be reunited with her daughter.

How could Lily not feel for her?

The more she tried to imagine her mother returning to Provincetown and picking up the pieces of her life, while trying to find a way back to Lily, the more it hurt. Kelly hadn't started a new family to replace Lily. She had done it to try and bring happiness back into her life. Lily couldn't fault her for that.

The three of them fell silent and stared out at the water.

The next morning, they sat down for breakfast on the veranda and talked some more, sharing stories about their childhood and their children. When the afternoon sun began its descent below the horizon, bathing the world in

lyrimberly Thomas

hues of pink and purple, Sophia and Ian packed up and left.

Soon after they hit the road, her aunts showed up on her doorstep, cousins in tow, and with bags of food and drinks. Everyone talked over each other as they set up a table outside. By the time Lily was done greeting everyone, the kitchen counter was filled to the brim with food, and the silence she'd been dreading was filled with laughter and conversation.

Aunt Heather draped an arm over Lily's shoulders and steered her out onto the back porch, where her cousins were already sprawled over the beanbags and chairs and clinking their glasses together. "Did Ian and Sophia have a good time?"

Lily sat down across from her aunt Heather, and linked her fingers together. "Yeah, I think they did. I wish they could've stayed longer."

Aunt Heather eyed her over the wine glass. "They'll be back soon, I'm sure. How are you feeling about everything? I know it's a lot to take in."

Lily leaned back against the beanbag and blew out a breath. "I don't think I ever stopped to wonder how hard it must've been for her, for Kelly, I mean. My dad always made it seem like she left me on purpose, but the more I learn about her relationship with my father, the more I realize she didn't have a choice."

Aunt Heather's expressive eyes fell, and her bottom lip gave a slight tremble. "She hated having to leave you behind. Kelly even thought about going back a few times. Thankfully, Stu talked some sense into her, and once I managed to get in touch with your aunt Mae, it helped."

Lily nodded. "Thank you for reaching out to her."

Aunt Heather leaned forward and patted her hand. "I

86

had a feeling you wouldn't want to be alone when you messaged me. I hope it's okay we all came over unannounced."

Lily gave her aunt a wobbly smile. "Of course. It's exactly what I needed."

As difficult as it was to realize that it had been down to Lily or her mental health, Kelly had made the right choice. Lily tried to imagine being unable to leave Lance and his constant manipulating and demeaning behavior; the thought made knots form in the center of her stomach.

Lance had turned into a mirror image of her father, with all of the gaslighting and the constant head games. In front of the whole world, he'd been good at playing the doting husband and pretending like he worshipped the ground she walked on. In private, he'd chipped away at Lily's confidence, everything from her appearance and weight to how she spoke.

Staying with Lance hadn't even been an option for her once the verbal abuse and cruelty didn't stop.

And she didn't regret leaving him. Not one single bit.

Lily was a lot more like her mom than she thought, but the thought didn't bring her any kind of comfort.

Chapter Ten

"Are you sure this is okay?" Lily set her purse down on the floor and adjusted the straps of the robe.

Sabrina stood across from her, near a window that overlooked the backyard. Behind a hand-painted screen door, the masseuse stood, preparing her essential oils.

The smell of incense rose through the air.

Sabrina looked over at Lily and waved her comment away. "Of course, it's okay. I like to indulge in massages too. They're incredibly relaxing."

Lily frowned. "I feel like I'm taking advantage."

Sabrina moved away from the window and pulled out her phone. "Not at all. Enjoy the massage, and let's talk after."

On her way out of the room, Sabrina paused to give Lily a smile over her shoulder. Then she pulled the door shut behind her, leaving Lily alone in the cream-colored, spacious room with a concrete slab in the center, a bathroom off to one side, and the vague silhouette of the petite masseuse with a bright smile and dark hair in an elaborate braid on top of her head.

Lily wasn't sure it was a good idea, but she couldn't deny the appeal of a massage, especially after the way her muscles ached after her run.

With a sigh, she let the robe flutter to her feet. She scooped it up into her arms, hung it up behind the door, and lowered herself onto her stomach. Clad in a thin bikini bottom and bra, with her arms out on either side of her, Lily felt more than a little ridiculous and nervous until the masseuse stepped out from behind the screen door, carrying a bottle of oil in her hand.

The soft strings of music played in the background.

Squirting a generous amount of oil onto Lily's back, the masseuse's fingers began to glide. Her fingers were soft and featherlight, starting at Lily's feet and working their way up to the shoulders. The masseuse lingered there, applying pressure at random intervals. Little by little, Lily began to relax, her muscles unwinding completely till her eyes squeezed shut. By the time the masseuse climbed onto the slab and dug her elbows into Lily's lower back, her entire body had gone slack.

She could definitely get used to this.

Sometime later, with no real sense of time or where she was, the masseuse tapped Lily on the shoulder and smiled at her. Slowly, Lily sat up and took the robe that was held out for her. In a daze, she stepped into the connecting bathroom and reached for her clothes. When she emerged, the room was empty, and her entire body was humming with energy. She smiled, stepped out into the dimly lit hallway, and made her way toward Sabrina's office on the far end.

Sabrina had an entire floor dedicated to the spa, with

a room for each treatment and a spacious bedroom in the center for clients waiting between treatments. Each room had two large windows overlooking the backyard and a clear view of the water sparkling in the distance. While Lily still couldn't imagine herself working in a place like this, she was nonetheless impressed with how Sabrina ran her business.

So far, Lily hadn't come across a single disgruntled client.

With a smile, Lily came to a stop outside Sabrina's office and knocked. Moments later, she pushed the door open and stepped into a small office with shelves of books on either side, a desk with a window overlooking the view, and a small bathroom to her right with tile floors. Sabrina sat behind her desk, phone pressed to her ear as she twirled a lock of hair around her fingers. She said something into the phone before gesturing to the chair opposite her desk.

Lily sat down and placed her purse in her lap. "I can come back later."

Sabrina shook her head and ended the call. "Don't worry about it. Just touching base. So, how was your massage? You look much more relaxed."

"Helga is incredible," Lily admitted, pausing to sag against the chair. "My body feels like jelly."

Sabrina chuckled. "That's how you know she's done a good job."

Lily nodded. "I can definitely see why clients are clamoring for her. Does she only do massages, or how does it work?"

"She is our in-house masseuse, but she's also a trained physical therapist."

"That's impressive. And you mentioned you've got a trained manicurist, as well?"

Sabrina sat up straighter and linked her fingers together over the desk. "Everyone here is certified or in the process of being certified. We cover the cost of the certification, provided the employee agrees to work for us for a certain number of years."

"What about your dermatologist?"

"Flexible hours. She's got her own clinic in Provincetown and is here by request," Sabrina replied. "I know it's an unusual way to run the business, but it's been working out for us so far."

"I'm sorry about all the questions," Lily offered with an apologetic smile. "I just want to get a better feel for things before I make a decision."

"No need to apologize. I get it."

"I can't really imagine working anywhere full time," Lily admitted after a brief pause. "I wanted to have more time to work on my book, so if I do come to work here, would you be all right with it being part time?"

Sabrina paused, and her expression turned thoughtful. "So, you'd be here on a need basis? Yeah, we can work with that."

Lily shifted from one side to the other. "Are you sure? I'm still trying to figure everything out here, so I'm not sure if I can commit to anything more right now."

Sabrina smiled. "Yes, of course. I completely understand. Whatever I can do to help you make your decision."

Lily opened her mouth to respond and was interrupted by the shrill ringing of her phone. She fished it out of her purse, saw Lauren's name flash across the screen, and frowned. When she answered the call, Lauren's voice was garbled and indistinct. She offered Sabrina an apologetic smile, stepped out into the hallway, and drifted closer to the window.

Out of the corner of her eye, she saw a small, dark-haired woman hurry past and duck into Sabrina's office. Whispered conversation spilled out into the hallway, punctuated by a sniff. Then the woman hurried back out, head hung low and eyes red-rimmed. Lily sent Lauren a message and went back into the office, only to find Sabrina standing near the window, a furrow between her brows and lips pulled down in a frown.

"Is everything okay?"

"Olive Vasquez is one of our employees. She's been having a hard time lately," Sabrina replied without looking at her. "I wish there was more we could do to help her."

Lily cleared her throat. "Vasquez? Is she related to Ben?"

"She's his sister," Sabrina replied with a sigh. "Sometimes, I think men should come with warning signs, you know. So, women know what they're getting themselves into."

Lily frowned. "It would be a lot simpler. Is there anything I can do to help?"

Sabrina sighed again and moved away from the window. "Not unless one of your cleanses can help a mother cope with the loss of a child and having to be married to an abusive man."

Lily paused and tried to choose her words carefully, knowing how sensitive the topic was. She licked her dry lips and shifted from one foot to the other. "She should leave him."

Sabrina sat back down behind her desk and buried

her face in her hands. "She already has, but leaving isn't just walking out the door. And Olive hasn't been the same since the loss of her son."

Lily lowered herself into the chair. "Can I ask what happened?"

"He was run over by a car," Sabrina said in a quiet voice. "Olive's relationship with her husband has always been volatile, but I don't think she imagined it would end up like this. She took her eye off of her son for one second, and he ran out into the street."

Lily sank into her chair and ran a hand over her face. "That's awful. I can't imagine having to survive something like that."

"Neither can I."

Silence settled between them.

Lily had no idea what to say next. While she knew what it felt like to endure an abusive husband and how it felt to try and leave that life and the person she was behind, she didn't know the first thing about losing a child. Couldn't imagine the kind of pain it brought or the strength it took to be able to pull herself out of such a place.

The conversation afterward was strained and trailed off.

On the walk back home, she couldn't stop thinking about Olive Vasquez—everything she had to go through and the sheer amount of will it must take to get out of bed in the morning. When she pushed the door to the house open, Lily lingered in the doorway and wondered what she would've done if she were in Olive's shoes.

Leaving Lance was the hardest thing she'd ever had to do, but she tried not to look back or remind herself that it had taken years.

What did it feel like for Olive?

Was the whole town filled with memories of the life she could've had, and the son who had been cruelly ripped away from her?

After changing out of her clothes and into sweatpants and a hoodie, Lily found herself on the back porch with a glass of wine in one hand and a blanket in the other. The sun was beginning to dip below the horizon, a kaleidoscope of colors stretching out as far as the eye could see.

She settled against the chair, draped the blanket over her lap, and took a long sip of her wine. It burned a path down her throat before settling comfortably in the pit of her belly. Then she traced the edges of the shoebox containing letters from her mom and her aunt Heather. After a few more sips of wine, Lily squared her shoulders and took out a letter at random, her heart missing a beat when she saw her mother's name scrawled at the bottom.

My dearest Lily,

I can't believe I missed your sixth birthday party. I wanted to be there. I begged your father to tell me where it was; I even told him I'd stand outside just to catch a glimpse of you through the window, but he refused.

Every day spent away from you breaks my heart. I thought that getting away from Eric would be the hardest thing I'd have to do, but I was wrong. Leaving you behind is my biggest regret, Lily, and I know you can't understand it right now.

What kind of mother leaves her child behind?

But I knew I couldn't stay. Not if I wanted to get better for you. Not if I wanted to give you a better life, and I tried. I tried so, so hard to bring us back together, but I failed. I want you to know I did fight for you. I fought long and hard, but your father is a powerful man, and he's got friends everywhere. But I don't want you to hate him, Lily.

Someday, I hope he'll see he's wrong.

In the meantime, I'll keep doing everything I can to fight for you. Someday, when you're old enough to read this, I hope you understand. I never wanted to leave you. You're my whole heart, my whole world, and the reason I get up in the morning. On the day you were born, when I held you in my arms, I knew you were the best thing that ever happened to me.

I'll keep dreaming of you till I see you again.

I love you with all of my heart,

Mom

Lily's heart felt heavy as she clutched the letter to her chest, tears streaming steadily down her cheeks. The crack in her heart unfurled and grew, the yearning and longing she felt for her mother almost overshadowing everything else.

Slowly, she rose to her feet, left the blanket and glass of wine downstairs, and climbed up the stairs to her room. In her bed, she curled up, the letter still clutched to her chest, and fell asleep.

In her dreams, she was six years old again, but this time, her mother was there, smiling at her from across the birthday cake.

Chapter Eleven

Bright sunlight danced behind her eyelids.

Somewhere in the background, she heard the shrill ringing of her phone.

Lily forced one eye open, then the other, spots dancing in her field of vision. She groaned, brought both hands up to her face, and buried her head in them. Then her arm flailed at her side till her fingers closed around her phone.

There was a low pounding in the back of her head when she pressed the phone to her ear. "Hello?"

"Good morning."

Lily sat up and pried one eye open. She winced and squinted. "Liam? What's wrong? Is everything okay?"

"Yeah, don't worry. I just wanted to check on you."

Lily ran a hand over her face and peered at the clock on her nightstand, realizing it was still six in the morning. "You're never up this early."

"I thought I'd take a chance and see if you were."

Lily yawned and sank lower against the mattress. "I got to sleep pretty late. There's some kind of weird noise coming from the bathroom downstairs, so it kept me up."

"You should have someone take a look at that."

Lily yawned again and blinked. "I'll try to do that today. Hopefully, it's nothing serious. How are things at work?"

"You know how hectic it can get. I've still got that high-profile case I'm working on."

Lily stumbled out of bed and drew the curtains shut. "Still keeping you up at night?"

Liam exhaled, and she could hear the rise and fall of conversation in the background. "Sometimes, but I think I've figured it out."

"You should trust your instincts, sweetheart. That's why you're in school to become a lawyer, honey. You'll figure out what needs to be done."

Liam's voice was muffled, and it drifted off. When he came back on, he sounded clearer than before and a lot more winded. "Thanks, Mom. I appreciate the vote of confidence."

"Always, sweetheart. How's Laura?"

"She's going crazy trying to plan the perfect wedding. The other day I tried to remind her it's still six months away, and she gave me the dirtiest look I've ever seen. I swear I thought I was going to melt into a puddle."

Lily chuckled and shuffled into the bathroom. She set the phone down on the desk, put Liam on speaker, and peered into the mirror. "You know my offer to help still stands, whatever you want."

"I'm not sure how much you can do from Province-town, but I'll let Laura know."

"Please do." Lily cupped her hand underneath the faucet and splashed cold water on her face. "Other than

97

that, how's everything else? Isn't your dad working on that big case with you?"

"I come in at a different time, and if we have to be in the same room, I usually sit on the far side of it," Liam replied, a stiffness in his voice. "It doesn't make working on the case easy, but I don't care."

Lily patted her face dry. "Sweetheart, I know you're mad at him, but he's—"

"I know, I know. He's still my father, and I get that but, Mom, I'm allowed to be angry after what he did to you. He spent years treating you horribly and cheating on you; that's not something I can just forget."

Lily stood up straighter and frowned at her phone. "Liam, he's still your father. Regardless of what happened between the two of us. You need to remember that."

"I know he's my father, but it doesn't mean I can't still be mad at him."

Lily sighed and gripped the edges of the sink. "As long as you don't stay mad for too long."

"I'll try," Liam promised. "Anyway, look, I'm back at home. I've got to go wake Laura up for work. I really miss you, Mom, and I hope everything is going okay there."

"It's going great, sweetheart. Have a good rest of the day. I'll talk to you later, okay? Love you."

"Love you too, Mom."

As soon as the line went dead, Lily pulled the phone away from her ear and set it down on the shelf on top of the sink. She continued washing her face, brushed her teeth, and changed into a pair of shorts and a sleeveless top. Then she snatched her phone off the shelf and tucked it into her pocket. On her way out the door, she paused to grab a banana off the kitchen counter.

When Lily returned to the house an hour later, she

was drenched in sweat and feeling much better than she had when she woke up. After a quick shower, she changed into a pair of jeans and a T-shirt and gathered her hair up into a bun on top of her head. She settled into a brisk pace and made a beeline for the inn.

The people of Provincetown were already wide awake and starting their day. A few of them even greeted her by name on the way past.

A small smile hovered on her lips as she stuck her hands in her pockets and continued her walk. Once she reached the inn, she pushed the doors open and was met with a blast of warm air and the smell of cinnamon and apples. Her stomach grumbled in response, but she ignored it and walked up to the main desk where her aunt Rebecca's daughter-in-law, Alice, sat.

As soon as Alice saw her, she stood up and smoothed out the front of her shirt. "Hi, Lily. It's good to see you again."

"It's good to see you too."

"Rebecca isn't here yet. She's having a bit of a late start this morning. Is there anything I can do to help?"

"I'm not sure. I wanted to ask her if she knew any good handymen to come take a look at something in the house. The bathroom downstairs is making this weird noise."

Alice paused and glanced over her shoulders. "Hold on, let me ask Tiana."

A woman with streaks of silver in her red hair and long, manicured nails poked her head out from the room in the back, her brows furrowed. "Did someone call my name?"

"Yeah. Tiana, this is Lily Alrich. She's Rebecca's niece. Lily, this is Tiana, the desk manager."

Tiana stepped out of the office, her entire face lighting up. "I was wondering when I'd get to meet you. Everybody's talking about you already. It's nice to meet you, Lily."

Lily gave her a warm smile. "Thank you."

"Lily wants to know if you know anyone who can take a look at the bathroom at the house."

Tiana nodded. "That'll be Ben. He can fix anything. He's right outside if you want me to get him."

Lily pushed herself away from the counter. "No, that's okay. I can go and find him. Thank you for all your help."

"Have a lovely day," Tiana called out to her retreating back.

Lily adjusted the strap of her purse and hurried through the back door, spilling out into the backyard, with lush greenery on either side of her. Ben was on the far side of the yard atop a ladder, a look of fierce concentration etched onto his face.

"Hi," Lily greeted when he looked at her. "Sorry to interrupt. Tiana mentioned you could help me with a problem I have."

Ben hopped off of the ladder and wiped his hands on a rag he took out of his back pocket. "I'm afraid the restaurant is full. I can't use my connections to get you a table."

"That's too bad. I heard you were the man to talk to about those things."

Ben laughed, and his entire face transformed, giving him a more youthful look. "I think someone's definitely been misleading you. I'm not that good."

"You sound like you can hold your own."

Ben put the rag back in his pocket and straightened his back. "A man's got to know what his limits are."

Lily studied his face, bathed in the soft light of the early morning sun. "I agree. So, does plumbing fall within your limits?"

"Plumbing?"

"The bathroom downstairs is making this weird noise," Lily explained, her hands fluttering at her sides. "I'm sorry to bother you with this, but I don't know who else to ask."

"Let me put the ladder away, and I'll come take a look."

Lily blinked. "It doesn't have to be right now."

"I don't have anything to do for the rest of the day. I'm sure they won't mind."

Before she could protest, he hurried off, carrying the ladder as if it didn't weigh a thing. She went back into the inn and lingered in the reception area, receiving a few odd looks from the clients. When Ben returned, he had washed some of the dirt off his face, and his dark, curly hair was slicked back.

In silence, they walked back to her house, shoes crunching against the gravel and the warmth of the sun on the back of their necks.

As soon as they reached the house, Lily gave him a quick tour, paused outside the guest bathroom, and folded her arms over her chest. "Do you think it's something to do with the infrastructure of the house?"

"We'll find out," Ben replied, his face giving nothing away. "Got any tools I can use?"

Lily nodded and unfolded her arms. She rummaged underneath the sink and found a box of tools her aunts had left behind. Ben was on his hands and knees underneath the sink when she returned. He offered her a grateful smile, propped the toolbox open, and let out a low whistle.

"That's a nice tool set you've got here."

Lily lingered in the doorway, a flush rising up her cheeks. "It's not mine. My aunts left it here for me. I don't think I've ever even used tools. My husband—my *ex*-husband—usually hired people to do this sort of thing."

Ben picked up a wrench and examined it. "It is usually better to hire a professional, especially if you don't know what you're doing. I bet you had your pick of the crop in New York."

Lily shrugged. "I guess you could say that."

"Do you miss the city? Sorry, people like to gossip around here, and you're the most exciting thing to happen in a while, so people have been talking about you."

Lily tilted her head to the side. "Oh, I didn't realize people were going to find me interesting."

"The Wilson family's long-lost niece returned at last? Oh, yeah, people are eating it all up. People can't get enough of the story."

Lily laughed. "I think they might've built it up too much."

Ben flashed her a quick smile before returning to the sink. "It'll die down, don't worry."

"You sound like you've got some experience with that."

"Yeah, when my sister and I first moved here, everyone was interested. Especially when I ended up marrying a tourist who came here on vacation with her family."

Lily's heart dropped. "You're married?"

"I was," Ben replied, his brows furrowing together. "Got a daughter too."

A short while later, Ben stood up and fiddled with the faucet. He listened carefully before nodding to himself. "Okay, it wasn't a pipe issue; that's the good news. The bad news is I'm not sure I fixed it. I might have to come back again."

"That's fine. I appreciate you coming to look." Lily stepped out and held her breath when he brushed past her. "Can I get you something to drink? I think I've got some beer and lemonade in the fridge."

"I'd love some lemonade."

When Lily came back out, carrying a tray with a pitcher of lemonade and two glasses, Ben was on the back porch, leaning over the railing. "Thank you again for coming to take a look."

Ben spun around to face her and smiled. "You're welcome. So, you never answered my question."

Lily set the tray down and straightened her back. "I didn't? Which one was that?"

"About the city," Ben replied, pausing to pour them both a generous amount of lemonade. "Your kids live there, right?"

"They do, but I don't miss New York as much as I thought I would. How about you? Does your daughter live here?"

Ben cleared his throat. "She does, but I don't get to see her much. I wasn't the best father to her growing up, so we don't have a good relationship."

Lily's stomach dipped at his words, trying but failing to imagine the man in front of her as a bad father. She didn't know him well enough to form a complete picture yet, but everything she knew contradicted what he'd said. She was having a very hard time reconciling his words to the image she'd formed of Ben as a kind, caring, and thoughtful man.

Finally, she snapped her mouth shut and was careful to keep her voice smooth and even. "I'm sorry to hear that."

"I'm sorry about your husband," Ben offered, eyeing her over the rim of his glass. "I guess life doesn't always work out the way we want it to, huh?"

Lily reached for her own glass and took a long sip. "Tell me about it."

Chapter Twelve

Lily pushed the windows open and sucked in a huge lungful of warm spring air. She was relieved by how warm it had gotten, but she still couldn't believe it was the second week of May already.

Where had all the time gone?

It felt like she'd blinked and had woken up in Provincetown, surrounded by her mom's family while rebuilding her life from scratch.

With a sigh, she went back into the room and realized her phone was vibrating on the dresser.

She picked it up, saw her aunt Heather's name flash across the screen, and frowned. "Hi, is everything okay?"

"Lily, honey, thank God. I've been trying to get a hold of you. I need your help."

"Are you okay? What's wrong?"

Aunt Heather said something to someone in the background, and her voice came back on, sounding frantic and on the verge of panic. "We need your help at the inn. I know you aren't a chef, and you don't have experience working at a restaurant, but we need help, any kind of help."

"Aunt Heather, slow down." Lily shoved her feet into a pair of sneakers and snatched a sweater from her closet. "Start at the beginning; what's going on? Why do you need my help at the inn?"

"Our sous chef quit," Aunt Heather replied, her voice rising toward the end. "Without warning, I might add. Angie is slammed and can't manage the lunch rush on her own. I don't know who else to call."

Lily grabbed her purse off the dresser and hurried out of her room. "Of course, I'll come and help. I mean, I'm not a chef or anything, but as long as that's okay with you."

Aunt Heather breathed a sigh of relief. "Of course, it's okay. You're used to doing this sort of thing as a dietician, right?"

"Making food isn't really something I've done for my clients," Lily replied gently. "But I have been looking up healthy recipes for my book. I'm on my way anyway."

"You are a godsend, sweetheart. Thank you."

Lily heard a loud commotion in the background, and her aunt's voice cut off. She pulled the phone away from her ear, realized the line was dead, and sighed. Then she hurried out the front door and in the direction of the inn. By the time she arrived, the kitchen was in an uproar, with Angie on one side raking her fingers through her hair, and the rest of the kitchen staff looking harried and drenched in sweat on the other side.

"The cavalry is here," Lily joked, pausing to peel off her sweater. She rolled up the sleeves of her shirt and glanced around. "Put me in, coach. I'm ready."

Angie choked back a laugh and threw her arms

around Lily for a hug. "You have no idea what a lifesaver you are right now. Thank you so much."

Lily drew back and touched two fingers to her temples. "Aye, Aye, Captain. Tell me what you need."

Angie withdrew and spun around to face the rest of the staff, all of them looking at her intently. "Okay, everybody, listen up. This is my cousin, Lily. You've all met her already. She's going to be helping out as my sous chef. It's all hands-on-deck here. We've got a busload of hungry people out there."

Lily's brows furrowed together. "Busload? Is that some kind of euphemism for something?"

Angie looked back at her and grimaced. "No, I wish it was. My sous chef picked the wrong day to leave me high and dry, not that it's ever a good time. We've got a bus full of football players passing through, and they all want their food to go."

Lily took the apron Angie handed her and tied it around her waist. "Let's not waste any more time then. What do you need?"

"Can you chop up those vegetables and pan-sear the burgers and chicken? I'll take care of the rest."

Lily nodded and stood behind the stove. While she worked, she let the hustle and bustle of the kitchen wash over her, everything from the smell of grease and cooked meat to the steady stream of waiters coming in and out of the kitchen, emerging even more red-faced each time.

It wasn't long before Lily was fanning herself and drawing her bottom lip between her teeth. Now and again, Angie came over and issued a set of instructions before she disappeared again.

Voices rose and fell around them.

A loud crashing sound brought Lily to the present

with a jolt, and she glanced over her shoulder in time to see Ben crouch low and grab trays off of the ground. "That's my bad. Sorry about that, everyone."

"Don't worry about it," Angie replied without looking up from the food. "Just try to be more careful."

"Yes, sir. I mean, boss." Ben rose to his feet and offered Angie a quick smile. He glanced over at Lily and raised an eyebrow. "I see you got roped into this too. How'd you get lured here?"

"Aunt Heather told me she needed me," Lily replied, pausing to flip the burger over. "I thought you were the caretaker here."

Ben hoisted the trays back up and set them down on the counter. "I am, but I'm also handy in a tough spot, so Alice recruited me."

Lily smiled. "Sounds like you're exactly the right person to have around in a sticky situation."

Ben leaned against the counter and blew out a breath. "I don't know about that. I think I've just gotten lucky."

"Sounds like more than luck. Sounds like hard work to me."

And a lot of consistency.

Not only was Ben in charge of the day-to-day maintenance and repairs done around the inn, but he'd explained he was also responsible for booking outside contractors in the event of any major repairs. In addition to ensuring the lighting and alarm systems were working properly and checking that doors and windows worked well at all times, Ben also helped out wherever and whenever it was needed. Although Lily herself couldn't imagine being responsible for so many things, she also couldn't imagine being as handy as Ben was.

He was useful as well as friendly.

And Lily found herself wondering why things didn't end up working out with his ex-wife. A part of her wanted to ask why the two of them weren't still together, especially when they had a daughter, but the other part of her wasn't sure she wanted to.

The fact he worked for her aunt had everything to do with it and then some. She didn't have time to like anyone, much less someone she was going to be interacting with on a regular basis. And Lily wasn't sure she trusted herself, not when what happened the last time she trusted a man was still fresh in her mind.

Would Lance's ripple effect ever fade?

With a slight shake of her head, Lily pushed the thought away and returned to the task at hand. Over the next two hours, Lily prepared as many meals as possible, alternating between cooking and helping Angie set the plates up. The entire time, she was keenly aware of Ben sneaking glances at her. Whenever she met his gaze, he smiled, and the butterflies in her stomach erupted.

Get a grip, Lily. You're not some lovesick teenager. You're here to work, not make goo-goo eyes at the caretaker.

And it wouldn't do her any good anyway.

Granted, the two of them had spent hours on her back porch the other day, talking about anything and everything they could think of, but it didn't mean anything else would happen between them.

By the time the lunch rush ended, Angie collapsed into a heap on the nearest chair, and the rest of the kitchen staff lagged. Lily wiped her hands on the back of her jeans and offered her cousin a bright smile.

"I don't know how you do it all the time, but we did it."

Angie stretched her legs out in front of her and

exhaled. "I don't know how we do it either, but we definitely couldn't have done it without you."

Lily shrugged. "I barely did anything."

Angie pushed herself up to her feet and adjusted the folds of her apron. "I know this is sudden, but would you be willing to consider helping out in the kitchen?"

"I don't know, Angie. You need a professional."

Angie nodded. "And I'm going to start putting out feelers and asking around, but until then, we need someone to help."

Lily tilted her head to the side and paused. "I guess I can help out until a more permanent solution is found."

Angie squealed and threw her arms around Lily. She gave her a firm, tight squeeze before drawing away. "Thank you so much. You really have no idea how much it means to me, to all of us."

"It's nothing, really. I'm happy to help."

It also gave her a chance to spend more time with her cousin and get an up-close and personal look at how the restaurant was. It had nothing at all to do with the handsome caretaker who made her stomach do odd little somersaults.

Or at least that was what Lily kept telling herself.

She told herself it didn't matter that whenever he looked at her, Lily felt like she couldn't breathe or her heart missed a beat when Ben offered to walk her home. Lily was so focused on convincing herself the pull she felt toward Ben didn't matter that she didn't notice they'd arrived back at her house.

With a smile and a quick wave, she raced up the stairs to her door.

Inside, she slammed the door shut and leaned against it. She was still smiling to herself as she kicked off her shoes and set her purse down on the kitchen counter. Lily was filling up a glass of water when her phone began to vibrate, first at once, then a few more times.

When she rummaged through her purse and found it, it took her a few seconds to realize what the text from her sister, Sylvie, meant. Lead settled into her stomach, and disbelief raced through as she read Sylvie's message again; the words "thyroid cancer" and "Aunt Mae" floated around in her head. The glass she held in her hand fell to the floor with a crash, and Lily's knees gave out, forcing her onto the floor.

She read Sylvie's message over and over, the tears streaming steadily down her cheeks. Her chest felt tight, like someone was squeezing her insides and trying to force everything to the surface. It felt like her entire world had stopped spinning on its axis, and Lily was suddenly expected to learn how to spend the rest of her life trying to keep her head above water. It wasn't until she pushed herself back up to her feet and read the message again that she realized what it all meant.

Aunt Mae was gone, and Lily was expected back in New York.

Chapter Thirteen

"Hello? Is anybody home?"

Lily took a small sip of her water and cleared her throat. "I'm in the kitchen."

Aunt Rebecca emerged first, carrying a container of food and sporting a bright smile. Aunt Heather was right behind her, a bottle of wine tucked underneath one arm and a bag of groceries tucked under the other. The two of them set the stuff down on the counter and stood up to face her, their expressions going from pleased to concerned.

Aunt Rebecca set the container down and frowned. "What's wrong?"

Lily sucked in a harsh breath. "Sylvie, my sister... She messaged me last night and told me Aunt Mae is... She's gone."

Aunt Heather stepped out from behind the counter and reached for Lily. "Oh, sweetheart, I'm so sorry. What happened? The last time I spoke to her, she sounded well."

Lily's eyes filled with tears. "I don't know. She had

thyroid cancer, and she didn't tell anyone. That's all Sylvie told me."

Aunt Heather drew Lily into her arms and stroked her back. "She was a great woman. I wish we had been given the chance to spend more time together."

Lily sniffed and held on to her aunt for dear life.

Wordlessly, Aunt Rebecca joined the hug, and the three of them stood in the middle of Lily's kitchen, crying and hugging each other. When Lily felt a little steadier, she drew back and ran a hand over her face.

"I have to go back for the funeral, and I'll have to tell everyone where I've been."

Aunt Rebecca still held on to Lily's hand. "Would you like us to come with you? I'm sure we can move some things around if we need to. Your aunt Mae is the reason you found your way back to us; we'll always be grateful to her for that."

Aunt Heather nodded. "Absolutely. Whatever you need, we're here for you, honey."

Lily released a deep, shaky breath. "I appreciate that, but no. This is something I need to do on my own. Besides, I don't want to set my dad off any further. There's no telling what he might do if he sees either of you. Things are going to be tense enough."

Especially considering the two of them hadn't spoken since she hung up on him weeks ago. Since then, Lily had done her best not to dwell on what her father had done and everything he had taken away from her, but it was hard. Now, she felt everything rush back to the surface, including her anger at him for lying to her about Aunt Mae too. For years, he'd convinced Lily her aunt was conniving and scheming, and her only interest in life was to further her own gain and cement her status as a person of power.

Her father had even gone so far as to warn Lily about her aunt's interest in her and her life. For most of her life, she'd only been allowed to view Aunt Mae as a villain and had never once thought to question the lies she was being fed or the one-dimensional lens through which she had viewed everyone.

As usual, Lily felt like a complete and total idiot, one who had placed blind trust in someone who had been playing her like a fiddle all along.

Had anything her father ever told her been true? Or had her entire life been built on a foundation of lies?

For the life of her, Lily couldn't say.

All she knew was she'd been carrying around an ache in her heart since hanging up with Sylvie, and no amount of blaming her father made her feel better. If anything, it made her feel worse. In a short while, she was meant to be driving back to New York for her aunt's funeral, and she didn't even know what she was supposed to say to him. Or the rest of her father's family.

As far as she knew, they were as much to blame as he was.

With a slight shake of her head, Lily turned away from her aunts and rummaged through one of the cupboards. Her hands shook as she pulled out an empty glass and filled it with water. She downed it all in one gulp and filled it up again, her throat turning very, very dry.

Lily suddenly realized she had no idea what she was meant to do.

After setting her glass down on the counter, she picked up her phone and offered her aunts a grim look.

Then she wandered into the living room, scrolled through her contacts, and stopped at her father's name. On the fourth ring, her call went straight to voicemail, and she hung up.

She shouldn't have been surprised.

Eric Taylor was nothing if not a proud man, and even the death of his sister wasn't going to change that. Out of the corner of her eye, she saw her aunts exchange a quick, worried look. Then they joined her in the living room and pulled her onto the couch, allowing her to nestle comfortably in between the two of them. For a while, Lily sat there, letting them comfort her and pushing away all thoughts of New York and what awaited her when she got there.

She'd sold her house and moved out here for a fresh start. The last thing she imagined was returning weeks later and for a funeral, no less. Lily had assumed she'd be returning for Liam and Laura's wedding in six months' time.

With a gasp, she sat up and ran a hand over her face.

"What's wrong?"

"I need to tell the children," Lily murmured, her hand moving from her face to her hair. "I'm not even sure how to tell them."

"Were they close to her?" Aunt Heather rubbed her back and gave her a sympathetic smile. "It's better to tell them slowly and try to make sure they're sitting down or somewhere quiet to be able to process all of this."

A lump rose in the back of Lily's throat. "Sara was closer to her. They were getting to know each other better."

Aunt Rebecca stood up and cleared her throat. "Why

don't we step out onto the back porch and give you some privacy? We'll be here if you need us."

In silence, the two of them made their way outside, and the door clicked shut behind them. Through the screen door, she saw them lean over the railing and inch closer to each other.

Lily brought the phone up to her face and sank back against the couch. Her chest tightened, and her heart hammered against her rib cage as she settled on Liam's number and dialed.

He answered on the sixth ring, his voice thick with sleep. "Morning. Is everything okay?"

"You're at home, right?"

She heard some rustling and the sound of a door clicking shut. "Yes, what's wrong?"

"I'm going to call your sisters. I'll put us all in a conference call."

"Mom, you're scaring me."

Lily's throat closed up as she drew the phone away from her ear. Moments later, Lauren and Sara were both on the call, sounding equally confused and concerned. Lily stood up, scrubbed a hand over her face, and squared her shoulders.

"Your aunt Sylvie called. Aunt Mae died last night."

Sara gasped. "I thought she was doing better. She told me she was feeling better."

Lily swallowed. "You knew about the cancer?"

"She didn't want me telling anyone," Sara whispered in between sharp intakes of breath. "Oh, Mom. I'm so sorry. I knew you were just getting to know her too."

Lauren exhaled. "When's the funeral?"

"Day after tomorrow," Lily whispered, pausing in

front of the back door. "I'll be driving down in a few hours once I get the house locked up."

"We'll have the guest room ready for you," Liam told her in a quiet voice. "Do you want me to come down and get you?"

Lily shook her head. "No, it's okay. I could use the distraction."

Silence stretched between them.

"I'll see you all very soon."

Nearly seven hours later, Lily pulled up outside her son's brownstone—a red brick townhouse nestled on the city's outskirts. She brought her car to a halt, leaned over the dashboard, and squinted, studying the house in the dying of the light. With its three floors and an immaculate tiny front lawn, it still retained some of its charming, old-world kind of feel.

It felt strange to be back in New York and not staying in her house.

On impulse, she had driven past it, surprised to feel a familiar tug in the center of her chest. Knowing it wasn't her house anymore had upset her more than she thought it would, considering she'd been the one to make the decision to pack up, sell the house, and not look back.

With a sigh, Lily stepped out of the car and slammed the door shut. Before she could open the trunk, the front door creaked open, and Liam emerged in the doorway, the spitting image of his father with his dark hair, angular face, and button-down shirt tucked into a pair of dark jeans.

Wordlessly, he took the front stairs and strode toward her.

Lily stared, her stomach giving an odd little dip when Liam reached her and took her into his arms. For a while, they stood in the middle of the street, with Lily clinging to her son and trying to commit his smell to memory. He smelled like spicy aftershave and lemon-scented soap, and it made some of the knots in her stomach unfurl.

When he drew back, he gave her a small smile. "It's good to see you, Mom."

Lily cleared her throat. "It's good to see you too, sweetheart. I'm sorry to be coming back under these circumstances."

Liam nodded and reached into her trunk, hoisting the duffel over his shoulders. "It's going to be okay. I don't want you to worry about a thing while you're here."

Lily saw a flash of movement, and Laura appeared in the doorway, a furrow between her brows. She lifted a hand up to her face and squinted at them. Then Liam ushered Lily up the front steps and into the house. In the doorway, she paused to greet Laura, who gave her a quick hug and hurried after them.

"If there's anything we can do to help," Laura began. "I made sure the guest room was in order. There are fresh towels in the bathroom, and I changed the bedsheets."

"Thank you," Lily murmured, pausing to lace her fingers behind her back. "I'm sorry about all of this."

Laura caught up to them and pushed the door to the guest room open with a creak, revealing a large room with cream-colored walls, a window that overlooked the backyard, and the smell of citrus-scented air freshener lingering in the air.

It looked exactly the same way it had the last time Lily had seen it.

Lily couldn't quite believe it was *she* who was different.

Slowly, she stepped into the room and wandered through it, picking up and setting down several things. "Have you gotten in touch with your father?"

Liam set her bag down on the floor. "Yes, I've spoken to him and Amy."

Lily nodded and twisted to face him. "And your grandfather?"

Liam nodded slowly. "He sounds okay, all things considered."

"I'm going to go make us some dinner and give you two a chance to talk," Laura announced with another quick look in Liam's direction. "Let me know if you need anything."

Once the door clicked shut behind her, Lily perched on the edge of the bed and sighed. "I can find a hotel if the two of you aren't comfortable with me being here."

Liam crossed over to her and sat down. "Mom, you were going to move in here; of course, we don't mind having you."

Lily stared at a spot on the wall. "Are you sure I won't be in Laura's way? I know she's been struggling with her interior design business lately and is trying to work from home."

Liam draped an arm over her shoulders. "Don't worry about any of that right now. I'm more worried about you."

Lily let out a deep, shuddering breath. "I just can't believe she's gone."

And she still couldn't believe how much time had

been wasted thinking that Aunt Mae only wanted to use her.

Suddenly, the thought of coming face-to-face with her father, with everything she knew, seemed like the most exhausting thing she could think of. Especially when all she wanted to do was curl up into a ball and cry herself to sleep.

Chapter Fourteen

Lily smoothed out the front of her blouse and twisted to the side, frowning at the dark circles under her eyes and the gaunt look there. When Liam came knocking on the door and poked his head in, Lily was peering intently into the mirror, a makeup brush in hand.

"Need a hand?"

Lily held his gaze in the mirror. "You don't need to hover, you know."

Liam shoved both hands into the pocket of his suit. "I know."

A heartbeat later, Lily stood up straighter and patted her hair. "We should leave soon."

"Laura made us some breakfast. I know you're not hungry, but you should try to eat something. You're going to need your strength today."

Lily spun around to face him and tucked her hand into the crook of his elbow. "I'll try."

In silence, he led her out into the hallway, which spilled out into the kitchen, where Laura stood on the other side of the counter, frowning. Once she saw them, she stood up straighter and moved to the stove. A heavy silence settled over them as Liam pulled a chair out for Lily and helped her sit down. Then Laura set out a few plates, a pan full of scrambled eggs, and a pitcher of orange juice.

Lily could barely hear past the pounding in her ears.

She pushed her food around, took a few bites, and stood up. "I'm going to use the bathroom and grab my purse."

Liam frowned at her and said nothing.

She felt his eyes on her as she retreated into the room. There, she brought her head to rest against the door and exhaled. Her hand trembled as she stepped into the bathroom and winced at the fluorescent lighting. Lily avoided looking at herself in the mirror and instead splashed cold water on her face and gripped the sink. While she had no idea if she was ready to see her father or anyone from his side of the family, she knew she couldn't walk away for Aunt Mae's sake.

With a resolute nod, Lily straightened her back and stepped outside, finding Laura and Liam by the doorway, dressed in all-black and sporting solemn and grave expressions. Liam placed his hand on the small of her back and led her outside. Laura looped her arm through hers and led her down the front steps. In the car, Lily sat in the front, with her purse nestled in her lap and bile in her throat.

The funeral went by in a blur, with Lily standing in a row of Taylors by the casket, many of their faces blurring together except for her father's. He stood near the casket, his head held high and a blank look on his face. Lily kept sneaking glances at him and frowned at the resolute way he shook people's hands. When he glanced over at her, she hastily looked away and stared at the stained-glass window above his head.

Early morning sunlight filtered in, casting tiny particles on the hardwood floors.

In spite of how early it was, both pews were filled, and a long line of well-wishers was already forming, all of them there to pay their final respects. Lily hardly recognized the people in the distance, but she found she didn't care. All she could think about was her dear Aunt Mae, fighting a losing battle against cancer that no one knew about.

First, Aunt Mae had lost her husband to lung cancer twenty years ago.

And now this.

Lily sniffed and dabbed her eyes with a tissue.

Out of the corner of her eye, she saw her father being pulled away by an older man in a faded suit with streaks of silver in his hair. The picture of solemnity and brevity, Lily could almost forget he and Mae had never gotten along to begin with. Since reconnecting with Aunt Mae, Lily had learned all sorts of things about her father's childhood, including the fact he had always believed himself to be superior to others.

Because of his superiority complex and his general distaste for women, he and Aunt Mae had never gotten along. Even as children, her aunt had steered clear of him, preferring to wash her hands of her brother, the man she had once declared to have a God complex. Seeing him now brought everything back for Lily, including her newfound knowledge of how he'd treated her mother.

And how he still treated Amy, her stepmother.

As if the mere thought conjured her, Amy Gruntle

emerged from behind a screen door, droplets of water on her face. In her knee-length black dress and with her hair piled on top of her head, she was the picture of sadness and defeat. And if Lily hadn't been looking directly at her, she would've missed the slow way she walked toward Eric and the flash of uncertainty when he looked over at her.

He was still the same hateful and domineering man he always was.

Lily had no idea why she imagined he had changed.

With a slight shake of her head, Lily moved out of the line and stepped behind the screen door. Once she pushed the door to the bathroom open, she ran straight into her aunt Evie, who was looking into the mirror and sniffing. Their eyes met, and Aunt Evie stepped away from the sink and held her arms open. Lily swallowed, stepped into her aunt's arms, and shuddered.

"You look good, honey," Aunt Evie said into her ear. "I see Provincetown's been treating you well."

Lily frowned and pulled away. "How are you holding up?"

Aunt Evie shrugged, but she wouldn't meet Lily's gaze directly. "I'll be all right, sweetheart. Don't you worry about a thing."

Lily searched her face, the frown still hovering on the edge of her lips. "You don't have to pretend to be strong, Auntie."

Aunt Evie's lips lifted into the ghost of a smile. "You haven't called me that since you were little."

Lily reached for her hand and squeezed. "I'm glad Kevin, Stacy, and Shawna are here."

Aunt Evie's expression grew grave. "I don't know what I would do without them or Jared."

Ever the peacekeeper, her aunt had done her best to avoid conflict in their ranks. Since she was a little girl, her earliest memory of her aunt Evie was of her wedging herself between Eric and Mae in an attempt to get them both to cool off. Now, at seventy-two and with three grown children, Lily had no idea what her aunt did with her time. Or how Evie was meant to cope with the loss of her only sister.

Her heart ached for her aunt Evie, especially when she tucked her hand into the crook of Lily's elbow, and the two of them stepped out. A cold breeze wafted into the church, carrying the scent of wildflowers and freshly mowed grass. Lily took Aunt Evie back to her husband and children, who sat in the back pew, vacant looks in their eyes.

They barely saw her when she greeted them.

Little by little, everyone trickled outside, and the last of the well-wishers left. Sara and Lauren stood on either side of Lily, who hovered in the back, unsure of what to do with herself. In silence, the remaining family members piled up into their cars and drove back to her father's penthouse, a few blocks away from the church. As soon as she stepped in through the front door, she lingered, memories of her last Christmas in the house hitting her all at once.

It was the Christmas she'd met Lance, and her whole life had changed.

From across the room, she saw her ex-husband engaged in a conversation with her stepmother, who stood with her back straight and a stiffness in her shoulders. Lily took a glass of water from a passing waiter and eyed Amy, who was steered away by her father. Moments later, she watched her stepmother freeze, and a panicked look marred her face.

Lily knew that look and had seen it all too well when she was growing up.

The great Eric Taylor was belittling his wife again—at his sister's funeral—to boot. Lily couldn't decide if she was surprised or resigned to the fact he hadn't changed one bit.

She drifted closer to a group of distant relatives and engaged them in small talk, but all she could see was her father's hand around Amy's waist and the cold look in his eyes. Eerily similar to the one he'd given her the day she announced she was going to become a dietician.

It was the same look of steely-eyed disapproval she'd spent all of high school trying to escape.

When Lily realized she'd been drawn into a conversation with her siblings, Aunt Evie, and her father, she came back to the present with a jolt. Her father cast a glance in her direction, and she didn't miss the tightness around his eyes or the hard set of his lips.

"I'm sure she'll be moving back soon," Eric was saying loudly and to anyone who would hear. "A reconciliation isn't too far off. I've already spoken to Lance about it."

Lily's blood turned to ice. "You talked to Lance about a reconciliation without asking me first?"

Eric waved her comment away. "Why would I need to ask you?"

Lily stiffened and squared her shoulders, hoping she looked more assertive than she felt. "Because it's my life, and you can't make decisions for me."

Not anymore, at any rate. Especially not when she knew he'd been behind the scenes all along, pulling the strings.

"This is not the time or the place for a conversation like this," Eric told her in a low voice. He gave her a hard look and stood up straighter. "Anyway, we can discuss the details later."

Lily took a step back and shook her head. "No, we can discuss this right now. I'm not going to let you rope me back into this...this toxic, twisted mess of yours. I'm not a child anymore, and I know better now."

And she was not going to be her father's puppet, not anymore.

Something in her had snapped at the news of her aunt Mae's death, and she wasn't ready to put the pieces back together, not if it meant they didn't fit anymore.

Even if that meant finally standing up to her father.

Eric's mouth pressed into a thin, white line. "Excuse me?"

"We should take this outside," Aunt Evie said with a quick look around the room.

She ushered everyone out onto the terrace and shut the door behind them, leaving the few remaining guests milling around and talking.

When she wheeled around to face them, Aunt Evie's face was flush with anger. "This is Mae's funeral. I know the two of you have your problems, but don't you think this isn't the time or the place?"

Shame, low and hot, burned in the center of Lily's stomach. "I'm sorry, Aunt Evie."

"You should be," Eric told her coldly. "This isn't how a daughter behaves."

Lily wheeled on him, and her mouth fell open. "But this is how a father behaves? You're not even sorry at all, are you? All you care about is the fact you can't control me anymore."

"Well, obviously, you've made a mess of things without me," Eric snapped, his eyes tightening around the edges. "Look at what's happened to you since I stepped back. First, your divorce and now moving to that ridiculous little Povertytown—"

"Provincetown," Lily corrected with a lift of her chin. Her face was growing hot with anger, but she didn't falter. "You know exactly what it's called, Dad. Don't pretend otherwise. That's where you and Mom met."

Eric's eyes narrowed further. "We don't talk about her."

"And since the great Eric Taylor has spoken, I suppose we should all fall in line, right? Because that's how it's always been. You think you know better, but you don't, Dad. All you do is try and make sure people are doing what you're doing. That's all you know."

Lance materialized next to her and placed a hand on her arm. "Lily, I think you should—"

"Get your hand off of me," Lily told him with a withering look. "I don't know how I didn't see it before, but you're just as bad as he is, so of course you would side with him. It shouldn't surprise me."

Lance folded his arms over his chest. "Your father isn't wrong about you being lost since the divorce. Really, Lily, isn't it time you came back to New York?"

Lily glanced between the two of them, heart hammering unsteadily against her chest. "Why? So, the two of you can control me again? I don't think so. I don't know why it took me so long to see it...all of the lying, scheming, and manipulating. The two of you should be ashamed of yourselves."

"Don't be hysterical—"

"She's not being hysterical." Lauren stepped forward

and gave her dad an angry look. "Don't talk about Mom like that."

"She has every right to feel the way she does," Sara added with a steely look around her. "Let's go, Mom. We don't have to be here for this."

"Son, tell your mother to calm down," Lance said, rolling his eyes. "This is not the place for one of her scenes."

Liam folded his arms over his chest. "Mom isn't a child, and I'm not your lackey."

With an angry look in his father's direction, Liam led them all back into the living room, where they earned a few curious looks. Before she got on the elevator, Lily caught a brief glimpse of her stepmother, who shrank under her father's withering stare. Then the doors pinged shut, and her children formed a half-circle around her. Downstairs, they all piled into Liam's car, and Lily's phone rang.

She sat in the back, wedged in between her daughters, and fished it out of her pocket. A short while later, they pulled up outside a restaurant a block away from Liam and Laura's place. As soon as they stepped in through the revolving glass doors, Lily saw her siblings at a table in the back, next to a window overlooking a park.

Sylvie and Lucas pulled her into a hug as soon as they saw her.

Then everyone sat down, pulling up chairs as they did. Once they were settled, Sylvie took Lily's hands in hers and squeezed. "How are you? We saw what happened with Dad."

Lily sighed. "I don't know what to do."

"He'll get over it," Lucas assured her from the other

side of the table. "He just needs time to get over the fact he can't control you anymore. You're an adult."

Lily gave him a strained smile. "I've been an adult for a while now."

"Yeah, but you know how he is. I know Judy is twenty-four and in university, but she'll always be my little girl. And I also get carried away sometimes, which Susan always likes to remind me of."

"So do I," Sylvie admitted after taking a long sip of her iced tea. "Stan was just telling me that I need to ease up. And June and Beth are always on me about being in their personal space and giving them room to breathe, but as parents, we can't always help it."

Lily reached for her own water and took a sip. "I guess."

Except, Lily knew her situation was different.

Her siblings were wonderful parents, and they had supportive partners. Lily, on the other hand, had been raised by a man who ruled with an iron fist, kept everyone around him in a state of terror, and manipulated her, to boot. A part of her couldn't help but wonder what her life would've been like if she'd ended up with a different parent. One who cared more about her than his own needs.

Next to her, Sara reached for her hand across the table and squeezed. "Grandpa shouldn't have done what he did, and Dad shouldn't have backed him up. Anyway, Mom, when are you headed back to Provincetown?"

"Trying to get rid of me already?"

Lauren draped an arm over her shoulders and squeezed. "Not at all. We're all really excited to plan our trip there. We can't wait to meet the Wilsons."

Lily glanced between her children and smiled. "I'm glad. I'm sure they'll all love you."

In spite of her jumbled-up emotions and the confusion she felt at calling her father out, Lily was relieved she still had something waiting for her back in Provincetown. Something that hadn't been tainted by her father's poison.

Chapter Fifteen

L ily laughed and twisted the steering wheel. "No, I'll be there soon, Grandma Jen." She paused and ran a hand over her face. "I didn't feel like there was too much traffic, no."

With that, she pulled the car to a halt outside her grandparents' house, a large two-story, Victorian-style mansion nestled on a cliff overlooking the water. When she got out of the car, she smiled at the wraparound veranda encircling the front and back porch and the immaculate lawn with a pristine white fence surrounding it.

Her grandparents emerged in the doorway, dressed in identical khakis and button-down shirts. Lily's heart soared as she kicked the door to her car shut and hurried over to them. Grandma Jen pulled her in for a hug and lingered, smelling like cinnamon and apple. Grandpa Frank, on the other hand, offered her a quick hug coupled with a pat on the back.

Both of them were beaming and acting like she'd been away for weeks.

"I'm just going to get my bag from the car." Lily's eyes didn't leave their faces as she walked backward.

She stopped at the trunk, hoisted the bag up, and set it down on the ground. Grandpa Frank draped an arm over her shoulders and led her inside into a spacious hallway with hardwood floors and a glittering chandelier.

With a hum, he steered her in the direction of the guest room, complete with a large bed, a closet over-looking it, and a window with a view of the sparkling water. Grandpa Frank offered her a wave, took his car keys, and left, the front door clicking shut behind him. She wheeled her bag into the room, ducked into the guest bathroom, and splashed water on her face. When she came out, Sophia greeted her in the doorway, pausing to admire her shorts and T-shirt.

Sophia draped an arm over Lily's shoulders and took her to the back porch, where a few more of her cousins sat. "Lil, I don't think you've met Suzie yet. She's Uncle Frankie's kid, and she works with her dad at the real estate company."

Lily offered her a small wave. "It's nice to meet you."

Suzie sat up and gave her a quick hug. "You too. Grandma Jen hasn't been able to stop talking about you. I've really been looking forward to meeting you."

Lily sat down on a beanbag with her back pressed against the wall. "You too."

Sophia sat next to her and made a sweeping hand gesture. "You remember Emily and Tara, right? They're Aunt Ashley's kids."

Lily nodded. "It's nice to see you both again."

"How was your trip to New York?" Tara reached for a chip and popped it into her mouth. "I've never been, but I've always wanted to go."

Lily shrugged. "It was okay. New York isn't for everyone, I guess."

And right now, it was tainted with her father's memories and lies.

He had ruined the city for her and everything she loved about it.

Lily turned to Emily and smiled. "Grandma Jen mentioned you own that bakery on the main street. What was it called?"

"Decadent Treats," Emily replied with a beam. "I love owning my own bakery."

"I bet. I stopped by there the other day, and it was packed. Luckily, I got the chance to try one of your croissants. You are, by far, the best baker I know."

Emily blushed and waved her comment away. "You're being way too nice."

"I mean it though."

"Why don't we all get started on lunch?" Grandma Jen appeared in front of the sliding glass door in an apron with her hair tied into a bun at the nape of her neck. "I'm sure everyone is hungry. I've got some lobster broiled with butter sauce ready for the oven."

Emily stood up and patted her stomach. "Grandma Jen, you know I'm trying to lose weight."

"Honey, you're in the wrong business," Grandma Jen told her with an indulgent smile. "And you love my lobster anyway."

Emily sighed. "I really do. Oh, well. I can start my diet tomorrow."

"Charlotte and Savannah are never going to let you hear the end of it," Tara teased, pausing to throw her arms around her sister. "It's a good thing they've got their aunt to tell them the truth about their mother's valiant battle to stay on her diet."

Emily scowled in her sister's direction. "What's in it for you?"

Tara clutched her chest. "It hurts me that you don't trust me, sis."

Emily raised an eyebrow. "It could have something to do with the fact that you've been pulling pranks on me for as long as I can remember. And you wonder why I don't trust you."

Sophia laughed and threw an arm around Lily's shoulders. "Come on, those two could be a while, and don't even get them started on Ruby."

"Ruby?" Lily stepped into the house and made a beeline for the kitchen, where a tray of fried clams, a plate of vegetables, and a separate plate of sea bass were already laid out. "That's Tara's daughter, right?"

Sophia nodded. "That's right. See, I told you that you'd have no problems remembering everyone."

"Don't tell them about my secret family tree sheet," Lily whispered, pausing to pick up the knife and stand behind the counter. "I want them to think I have an excellent memory."

Sophia chuckled and pretended to zip her lips shut. "My lips are sealed. They won't hear it from me. I don't even know anything about a family tree sheet."

Lily rummaged through the cupboards for a cutting board. When she found it, she set it down on the counter and picked up a knife. "Wait, remind me again, which one is Tara's husband?"

Sophia glanced up from seasoning the fish and frowned. "Tara doesn't have a husband. We don't even know who Ruby's dad is."

That poor girl.

Knowing Eric, as awful and horrible as he was, was better than not knowing who her father was at all.

Lily couldn't imagine what it must've been like for Ruby, so she offered a sympathetic frown. "That must be awful."

Sophia shrugged. "I don't know. Tara doesn't like to talk about it, and we don't want to push her. Someday, when she's ready, she'll tell us."

Lily sighed. "That's fair. What about Emily's husband? I can't remember what you told me about him."

Sophia glanced over her shoulders at the sisters standing on the back porch, helping their grandma with the grill. As soon as she glanced back at her, Lily wondered if she'd said the wrong thing. Since she was still getting to know them all, she knew she had to be careful. But she didn't feel like she had to walk on eggshells around the Wilsons, which was a big deal to her.

Having her sister confide in her like this touched Lily more than she knew how to put into words. Little by little, they were opening up to her and making her feel like a part of the family—in a way that made her heart feel full.

"Emily's husband, Trevor Ricker, died in a car accident not too long ago."

Lily's stomach dipped. "I'm so sorry to hear that. I can't even imagine what that must've been like for her."

"Thank God for her girls. They kept her going."

"Children have a habit of doing that," Lily agreed absentmindedly. She tucked that information away and returned to cutting the vegetables. "What about their brother...Jeff, was it?"

"Golden Jeff," Sophia mused with a shake of her head. "He's their mother's favorite. He's a construction worker, so he removes snow, works in construction, that sort of thing. He married his high school sweetheart, Tay, who is a florist; they have two beautiful kids, Jason and Maria."

Lily nodded to herself. "Nice. I'll have to mark them on my sheet."

"You're going to have to show it to me someday," Sophia joked, pausing to glance up at her, bright eyes glimmering with humor and mischief. "You should color code it or something."

Grandma Jen poked her head in. "What are you two whispering about? That food is meant for dinner."

Lily stopped chopping up vegetables and glanced over at her. "Dinner?"

Grandma Jen nodded. "Everyone is coming over later for dinner. We're having soft shell crab sandwiches and lobster."

Lily's eyebrows drew together. "Have I had that?"

She'd tried so many different types of food over the past few weeks that she could no longer remember. All she knew was everything was better and fresher than anything she'd ever tasted.

Her taste buds tingled in anticipation.

Sophia laughed, and the two of them stepped out onto the back porch, hand in hand. "All you have to do is add mayonnaise on it, and you'll love it."

"I'm not a fan of mayonnaise."

Sophia patted her hand. "You will be once you try it. Oh, and just wait till you try wicked oysters."

"Wicked oysters? Sounds like something out of a movie."

Tara bridged the distance between them and handed Lily a glass of lemonade. "It really does feel like it is.

They're cooked in their own juices to preserve their taste and texture. We should take you to get some. It's the best delicacy in Cape Cod."

Emily ruffled Tara's hair and made a face at her. "Is my sister trying to convince you that wicked oysters are the best delicacy in Cape Cod? Don't listen to her. She has no taste buds, so she can't be trusted."

Tara stuck her tongue out at Emily. "Can too."

Emily waved her comment away. "No, the best delicacy is lobster rolls. Imagine a roll of freshly steamed hot lobster meat mixed with celery and fresh mayonnaise and served on a warm, toasted roll."

Sophia shook her head. "No, you're both wrong. Fried clams are superior to both of those. Fresh clam meat, dipped in batter and deep fried to a crisp. Come on, tell me your mouth isn't watering at the mere mention of it."

Lily's stomach grumbled loudly, and everyone burst into laughter. Sheepishly, she draped an arm over her stomach and gave them all an embarrassed smile. "I think we can all agree that everything sounds delicious."

Grandma Jen emerged and steered them toward the barbecue. "You can debate while you help me make the food. Come on, put those hands to good use."

All four of them chuckled and set to work helping.

After a lunch of soft-shell crab sandwiches and iced lemonade, with the four of them taking turns regaling Lily with tales of their youth, they all stood up to help their grandma clean. When they were done, they all leaned over the railing, overlooking the ocean, and sighed.

Lily cleared her throat. "Are you really a nine-one-one operator?"

Tara giggled. "I am, but it's not as exciting as it

sounds. All I do is take calls, and I relay the reports to the appropriate law enforcement agency."

"It sounds plenty exciting to me. I've never met an emergency operator before."

Tara shrugged. "It's a lot less glamorous than it sounds. Emily is the one with the exciting job."

Emily snorted. "I make treats for people. What's so exciting about that? My girls are the ones who are going to change the world. One of them is a teacher, and the other is studying to be a doctor."

"You must be so proud," Lily said with a smile. "How old are they?"

"Charlotte is twenty-six, and she teaches drama at the local high school. Savannah is twenty-four and studying to be a doctor. She's got her sights set on orthopedics, but I think she'd make a good optometrist."

Tara choked on her drink and coughed. "Shame on you. You're just saying that so she can give you free eye exams."

"I am not," Emily replied with a lift of her chin. "And even if she does, I'm her mother. You're supposed to do things like that for your parent."

"It's called taking advantage."

Emily rolled her eyes. "It's called being a mom. I'm allowed to take advantage now and again, right, Sophia?"

"No, no. Don't put me in the middle. I know how this ends. So, Lily, when am I going to meet my nieces and nephew?"

"They're coming down for a visit next weekend," Lily replied with a smile. "They can't wait to meet you all, and they're all going to try and visit for Memorial Day for the get-together at my house."

Two hours later, when everyone came over for dinner,

and they all sat around the table, Lily kept trying to keep the frown off her face, and she tried to focus on everything she'd gained rather than let herself be weighed down by everything she'd lost.

The feeling stayed with her all through the night and well into the next morning as she drove back to Provincetown, the place she had come to think of as home.

Chapter Sixteen

"Hello?" Lily pushed the front door shut and left her bag by the door. She wandered into the house toward the sound of clattering in the guest bathroom. She set her purse down on the counter, glanced around, and found herself in the doorway, where Ben was sprawled under the sink, a wrench in his hand.

He looked up when he saw her and hit his head against the sink. "You're home early. I hope it's okay that your aunts let me in."

Lily shifted from one foot to the other. "Yeah, I drove straight here from Falmouth."

Ben rubbed his head and used a bandana to wipe the sweat off of his face. "How was your trip?"

Lily sighed. "Not as smooth as I would've hoped."

Ben tucked his bandana away and cleared his throat. "Do you want to take a walk along the beach?"

Lily nodded. "I'd like that."

In silence, they stepped out into the hallway together and made their way through the back porch and into the

Kimberly Thomas

crisp morning sun. Lily guided him down the path that led straight to the beach, and they fell into an easy rhythm. She shoved both hands into the pockets of her shorts and squinted into the sun-soaked distance.

The water glistened underneath the late morning light.

Ben paused to pick up a pebble and throw it in the water. "How was it being back? I'm sorry about your aunt."

Lily blew out a breath. "Thank you. I still can't believe she's gone."

Ben stood up straighter and cast a quick look in her direction. "Loss never feels real, you know. At least not in a way that makes sense."

"What do you mean?"

Ben's expression turned thoughtful. "I think the biggest problem with losing someone is not just accepting that you can't control it or it's a part of life; it's having to wake up in the morning and relive it all over again."

Lily swallowed, his words striking a chord within her. "Yeah, it's like it hits you again and again."

Here was a man who definitely understood loss deeply and intimately—who was still trying to process it.

It made Lily like him even more.

Ben twisted to face her, a sad smile on his lips. "Human beings are resilient though, so at least there's that."

Lily gave him a half smile. "At least there's that."

Ben turned so he was facing her completely. "I hope you don't mind me saying this, but from what I've heard, you're pretty resilient too."

"I don't know about that."

"I do," Ben replied with a small smile. "You should

142

give yourself some credit. Not a lot of people can go through what you did and come out on the other side."

Lily glanced out at the water, a strange fluttering in the center of her chest. "I don't know if I've come out swinging. Sometimes, it feels like I'm still being weighed down by the past, and a lot of the days, it feels really heavy."

"The past usually does," Ben murmured. "You want to know what I think?"

"Sure."

"I think when you get up every morning, you can choose how you'll react to what life throws at you, just like you can choose not to let the past weigh you down. I know it's a lot easier said than done, but it does help to think of things like that. At least it's helped me."

Lily tilted her head in his direction. "You've got a lot of insight about these things, huh?"

"When I lost my mom to cancer a few years ago, I thought nothing was ever going to be right again. So, I told myself to put one foot in front of the other, to just keep getting up in the morning and trying, and eventually, things would feel okay again, not in the same way, but enough that I could make my peace with it."

Lily touched his hand. "I'm sorry."

Ben cast a quick glance in her direction. "You shouldn't let your past define you. It's not all that you are."

"You shouldn't let your past define you, either." A jolt of electricity raced up Lily's arm. She snatched her hand away and let it fall limply to her side. "With your daughter, I mean."

Ben cleared his throat. "I don't know how to get

through to her or convince her I'm worth a second chance."

"I think the best thing to do is keep trying. Keep being consistent. Keep showing her that you've changed, and eventually, she'll see it too."

Ben pushed his hands into the pockets of his jeans and exhaled. "What if she doesn't?"

"She will," Lily replied without looking at him. "I know it's a cliché, but actions really do speak louder than words."

Ben made a noncommittal sound in the back of his throat and lapsed into silence. In the distance, a group of birds took to the sky, calling out to each other. Lily studied them, a smile hovering on the edge of her lips. Slowly, she rolled up the sleeves of her shirt and waded into the water.

Then she splashed Ben with water, and his mouth fell open into a comical O. Immediately, his expression changed, and he waded in after her. Lily shrieked and moved away from him. He caught up to her easily and splashed her back, causing her entire body to be soaked.

All at once, the two of them burst into laughter.

When Lily began to shiver, the two of them walked back to the house, a small berth between them. His hand kept brushing up against hers, making the butterflies in her stomach erupt. After handing him a towel to dry himself off, Ben took the rest of his tools and left. Lily stepped into the shower and caught herself humming the entire time.

Steam followed her when she came out of the room.

She was pulling on her shorts when she heard her aunts outside calling out to her. With a smile, she raced down the stairs and threw the front door open. As one, her aunts stepped forward and wrapped her in a hug, smelling of vanilla and cinnamon. Lily didn't realize she was crying until she sniffed and pulled away.

Aunt Heather ushered them all inside. "Why don't I make us all some tea, and we can sit on the back porch, and you can tell us about your trip?"

Aunt Rebecca took Lily's hand, soft and firm against hers, and led her outside. Side by side, the two of them sat, facing the water. Eventually, Lily brought her head to rest against Rebecca's shoulders. As soon as Aunt Heather came out, she sat down opposite Lily and placed a hand on her shoulder.

Lily sat up straighter and cleared her throat. "I'm fine."

"Honey, it's okay if you aren't," Aunt Heather told her, her eyes grave and solemn. "We know that you were just getting to know your aunt Mae, but it doesn't mean you grieve her any less."

Aunt Rebecca patted her hand. "Part of grieving is being upset over what could've been too."

A lump rose in the back of Lily's throat. "I just... I don't know why my dad kept her away from me for all these years. And seeing him didn't make me feel any better. It didn't give me any kind of clarity. If anything, it made things worse because all we did was slip right back into old patterns."

Lily had spent the entire fight with knots in her stomach and sweat forming on the back of her neck. It had taken her back to all of those endless fights in high school, all of the nights tossing and turning and praying for the day when she'd be able to leave.

Even thinking of it now left her with a bad taste in the back of her mouth.

Aunt Heather exhaled. "Your father will come around in time. He's just not the kind of man who's used to not getting his way."

Lily glanced over at her. "It's not an excuse."

"It's not," Aunt Heather agreed, her expression falling and eyes growing misty. "But there's nothing else to be done. I don't think you want to lose your father too."

"I don't think so either," Lily whispered, pausing to clasp her hands together. "But I don't know how to have a relationship with him now that I know the truth."

Silence stretched between them.

"And you should've seen him at Aunt Mae's funeral. He wasn't gloating or anything, but he was just...off."

Like it didn't bother him one way or another.

Lily's heart ached to think of what Aunt Mae would've made of his behavior.

Aunt Rebecca cleared her throat and looked out at the horizon. "Well, enough about that. Tell us about the rest of the weekend. How are Lauren, Sara, and Liam?"

Some of the knots in Lily's stomach unfurled. "They're really excited about coming down next weekend."

"We're excited to meet them," Aunt Heather told her before settling back against the beanbag. "Is there anything specific you want us to make for them? They do like seafood, right?"

Lily chuckled. "You don't have to worry about any of that. None of them are picky eaters, thankfully. But I'm going to need all the help I can get for Memorial Day weekend. I've never hosted this many people without professional help before."

Aunt Rebecca squeezed her shoulders. "We've got you, don't worry."

Lily snuggled against her aunt Heather and sighed. "Do you think it was a mistake for me to leave Lance?"

Aunt Heather drew back, and her brows furrowed together. "Who on Earth gave you that idea?"

"My dad," Lily replied, avoiding her gaze. "He made it sound like I was hysterical. Like I was crazy for leaving Lance and wanting something better for myself."

Aunt Rebecca stood up. "Honey, I'm sorry to say this, on account of him being your father and all, but he should want better for you, especially if Lance really was treating you the same way your father treats Amy."

Lily tilted her head back and looked up at her aunt. "Worse. I don't know how Amy can bear it."

And after years of defending Amy and being hung out to dry, Lily wasn't sure how to help anymore. She'd spent a lot of her childhood and most of her adolescence coming to Amy's defense against her father's cruel and callous comments about her weight, how she behaved, and everything in between. In the beginning, her father had been dismissive, as if she was little more than a fly on the wall, but over time, she'd begun to see behind the mask too.

Lily still shuddered to think of what she'd seen.

Was her father really past the point of redemption? Or was there still a chance for him to find his way back?

Aunt Rebecca leaned over the railing and clasped her fingers together. "Women can bear a lot more than you think. When we have to, I mean."

Lily stood up and joined her aunt at the railing. "We shouldn't have to, right?"

A soft smile hovered on the edge of Aunt Rebecca's mouth. "No, we shouldn't, but we do anyway. You were missed at the barbecue this weekend, by the way."

Lily bumped her shoulder against her aunt's. "I can't believe you all got together without me."

Aunt Heather laughed and came to stand on the other side of her. "There will be plenty more gatherings to come; don't worry."

"Speaking of gatherings, we ran into a few neighbors who were talking about you and Ben today." Aunt Rebecca twisted to face her, a knowing glint in her eyes. "The two of you have been getting along, huh?"

A flush crept up Lily's neck. "It's easy to talk to Ben. He's a good listener, and he offers a lot of great advice."

"And?"

Lily shrugged and pushed herself away from the railing. She stepped back into the house and went to the kitchen. There, she poured herself some lemonade and took a long sip before answering.

"And there's nothing going on between us. I just got divorced a few months ago. I'm not looking for anything."

Her aunts exchanged a knowing look.

"Just because you're not looking for anything doesn't mean it won't find you," Aunt Heather told her with a smile. "Ben is a good man, and he's been through a lot too."

Lily's fingers curled around the glass. "He has. I guess that's why he gives good advice."

Because his wisdom was rooted in pain, and it came from a place of familiarity. While Lily wouldn't wish that kind of hardship on anyone, she was glad Ben had made the most of things and was trying to turn his life around.

It made her like him all the more.

How could she not?

"We should go," Aunt Rebecca announced. "You've

had a long drive back, and I'm sure you want to get some rest."

In the doorway, they drew her into another group hug and lingered. Lily waited until they were a speck in the distance before she went back inside. She glanced around the empty living room, lingered on the half-empty bottle of wine, and took it upstairs with her. As she dimmed the lights and settled back against the covers, Lily couldn't help but reflect on all of the changes in her life so far, and wondered what she was meant to do next.

Chapter Seventeen

"**A**re you sure these streamers are okay? They look a little crooked." Lily placed both hands on her hips and frowned. "Maybe I should try something else."

"Mom, you've been up since six in the morning, and I've been on the phone with you for two hours; you need to chill." Sara's voice sounded amused and exasperated. She glanced out at her mom from the phone camera, a thin sheen of sweat on her forehead. "You do know this weekend is going to be great, right?"

Lily sighed. "I don't know. Maybe I built it up too much."

"I've seen you host a lot more people back at home," Sara reminded her with a laugh. "You're fine. You just need to find your footing."

"Footing?"

"Footing, groove. Whatever your generation calls it. You just need to get in the right headspace, I mean."

"Back in my day, you know, during the Great Depression," Lily joked, adopting a serious expression, "it was called finding inspiration."

Sara's laugh filled every corner of the house. "I didn't mean it like that, Mom. You know what I mean. Anyway, don't you still have time? Memorial Day is still on Monday."

"Today is Thursday," Lily reminded her with a shake of her head. "It's not enough time."

And she had no idea why she was so nervous about it all.

She'd hosted hundreds of parties over the years, with a revolving group of people coming in and out of the apartment. Over the years, Lily had cultivated her skills as a hostess and even found a cooking and catering crew that she'd been satisfied with. Although her parties in New York felt like a distant memory, belonging to another time and another person, she still recalled how it felt to bask in the afterglow of success. To have people's faces light up as a steady stream of food and drinks was passed out.

It was one of the few things she missed about her old life.

But she knew that in order to strike the right balance in Provincetown, she couldn't recreate the same atmosphere or even the same mood. Provincetown was, after all, a far cry from the glittering and polished lifestyle she led in New York City, surrounded by some of the city's most influential and powerful people.

"You're doing great, Mom," Sara interrupted, pausing to exhale. "Okay, listen, I've got to go. Jake's got this event he wants us to go to. I'll call you later, okay?"

"Okay, have fun. Be safe."

"Will do."

Lily was back on the ladder and hanging up a few more streamers when her phone buzzed. She took her phone from her back pocket and smiled when Sabrina's name flashed across the screen. Carefully, she climbed back down the ladder and sent Sabrina a response to her message.

A short while later, Lily was in the kitchen surveying her handiwork when the doorbell rang. She opened the door to reveal Sabrina in a knee-length blue dress with straps. As soon as her eyes landed on Lily, she placed the sunglasses on her head and smiled. Then Sabrina reached into her tote bag and pulled out a large bottle of white wine.

"I come bearing gifts."

Lily laughed and drew her in for a hug. "You didn't have to."

"I wanted to. You have a really nice place, by the way." Sabrina stepped in and glanced around, her eyes lingering on the back porch. "Talk about a breathtaking view. I'd be out there all the time if I were you."

Lily set the wine down on the counter. "I feel like I already am."

"Thank you for inviting me over." Sabrina set her bag down on the floor and glanced around. "I like the Memorial Day decorations."

Lily took out two glasses and poured them a generous amount of wine. "Thanks. You got any exciting plans for Memorial Day?"

"You mean besides a hot date with Netflix and the new Indian restaurant that delivers? That's pretty much it."

"You're not celebrating with your family?"

A shadow settled over Sabrina's face. "They invited

me, but I'm not going. I learned a while ago that their invitations are never just invitations. They come with too many strings attached."

Lily picked up their glasses and walked over to Sabrina. "What do you mean?"

Sabrina paused and stepped out onto the back porch. After she sat down, she pushed her hair out of her eyes and stared straight ahead. "You know how they say death and hardship will show you a person's true colors?"

Lily lowered herself onto the chair beside Sabrina and draped a blanket over her lap. "That's sad but true."

"When my dad died a few years ago, I realized his entire family was a bunch of hypocritical backstabbers, and all they wanted was to blame me for stuff. They blamed me for the money he left me; they blamed me for the property he left me. Basically, I got blamed, treated like dirt, and dragged through the mud, and because I didn't want to alienate them, I didn't do anything."

Lily touched Sabrina's shoulder and frowned. "I had no idea. I'm so sorry."

"Don't be." Sabrina took a long sip of her drink. "I know better now, but it still hurts, you know. Because I wouldn't have done any of that to them, and it sucks to know when it came right down to it, they didn't have my back."

"It's their loss."

Sabrina offered her a small smile. "Yeah, it definitely is, although my ex-husband would disagree with you. Then again, they did manage to turn him against me too, so his opinion shouldn't count for much."

Lily blew out a breath. "Sometimes, people really suck, don't they?"

Sabrina touched her glass to Lily's. "Pretty much. But now and again, they surprise you too."

"I'm sorry they put you through that. I can't imagine having to go through the loss of a parent and have people who are supposed to support you turn on you like that."

"Money and power have a way of changing people," Sabrina murmured between sips. "I heard you're not a stranger to the concept."

Lily snorted. "Definitely not. I don't know what made my ex change or think I wasn't enough, but it could've been the money and power. I guess he and my father really aren't so different after all."

Sabrina twisted to face her, the early morning sun slanted behind her. "No?"

"My father has been trying to control me my whole life," Lily explained with a frown. "He lied about my mom, about my aunt. It honestly makes me wonder what else he's lied about."

Sabrina's expression turned solemn. "I'm sorry about your aunt."

"You know what one of the worst things is? He lectured me during the funeral. It was his sister's funeral, and he still made time to be disappointed with me. I don't even understand how, and I'm not even sure why."

"Your dad sounds like a piece of work, no offense."

"He is," Lily agreed with a loud sigh. "And I don't know if I can forgive him for what he's done."

"Can I give you some advice?"

Lily nodded.

"I eventually forgave my family for what they did, but I haven't forgotten. I think it's human nature to forgive, but I think forgetting is a whole other thing. Forgetting means you haven't learned your lesson, so I think it's important to hold on to whatever this is meant to teach you."

Lily tilted her head to the side and studied Sabrina, everything from her heart-shaped face with a single freckle on the side of her mouth to the sadness lurking in the depths of her green eyes. When Lily glanced away, she took a long sip of her drink and sighed.

"Sorry, I didn't mean to bring the mood down," Sabrina offered. "But you're the first person in a long time who I've felt comfortable telling these things to."

Lily set her drink down and linked her fingers together. "Believe it or not, I feel the exact same way. You should come to the Memorial Day party. We'd love to have you."

Sabrina smiled, and it reached her eyes. "Thanks for the invite. I'll try to stop by. Your aunt was right, by the way. You and I are going to get along really well. I guess I should learn not to doubt Heather after all these years. She's a great judge of character."

"She really is," Lily agreed, with a laugh. "I hope I have half of her spunk when I'm her age."

"Heather gives us all a run for her money," Sabrina replied, pausing to stretch one arm over her head. "Did she ever tell you she used to be in a band?"

Lily's lips twitched. "Please tell me there are pictures."

Sabrina's eyes were glittering with humor and mirth. "I'm pretty sure your Grandma Jen still has some pictures and videos."

"Videos too?"

Sabrina leaned forward, and her expression turned serious. "There might even be a costume or two."

Lily burst into laughter. "Costume? What kind of band was this?"

"The kind you'd be embarrassed about fifty years later."

* * *

"I know I'm late. I'm sorry." Lily set down her purse and gave Angie a quick hug. "Sabrina and I were hanging out, and we lost track of time."

Angie wiped her hands on her apron. "She told you about Aunt Heather's band days, didn't she?"

"I had no idea Aunt Heather had such a...colorful life."

"Colorful is one way to put it. She's certainly been through some things. I could tell you some stories, but let's go through the menu for the weekend first."

Lily filled a glass of water and downed it all in one gulp. "Okay, I'm ready. Where do you need me?"

Angie beckoned her to the counter, where a few trays and a large notebook were laid out. "Okay, so I know we agreed we'd have a potluck with everyone from Provincetown, but there are a lot more people coming in from Falmouth, and I've been playing around with the menu."

Lily's eyes widened slightly. "That's a lot of food."

"It's a lot of people," Angie reminded her with a quick look in her direction. "Take a quick look and tell me what you think."

"Cob salads, charcuterie boards, finger foods, deviled eggs, chips, potato salad. Don't those last two kind of clash?"

"Uncle Frankie loves potato salad, won't eat anything without it, and some of the younger kids asked for chips."

Lily nodded and drew her bottom lip between her teeth. "Okay, that's fair. I get the clam chowder, lobster rolls, and oysters, but why are we making burgers and hot dogs when the rest of the menu is seafood-oriented?"

"In case anyone doesn't want seafood. With so many people involved, it's always better to have variety. Didn't you say you used to host parties this big?"

Lily glanced over at her cousin and smiled. "Yeah, but you guys are definitely more relaxed and have better food. Most of those events involved finger food or food dipped in weird sauces on an expensive plate. That sort of thing."

Angie patted her shoulders. "Don't worry. It's a good thing we've come to the rescue."

Lily laughed. "That's true. Wait, is that a chicken casserole dish I see on the list?"

Angie beamed. "It's one of my specialties. You'll love it."

"When do you need me to come by to help?"

"I don't need you to come here. I've got everything under control here. You'll need to be home to get everything sorted there. Didn't you mention your kids will be coming in on Saturday? You should spend time with them before the craziness of Sunday and Monday."

"Thanks, Ang."

"I'll take one of those cleanse programs you've got if you really want to thank me."

Lily gave her another hug and hurried out of the kitchen. "You've got it."

Chapter Eighteen

"You'll love the view, sweetheart, trust me," Lily murmured between sips of coffee. "I can't get over it."

"Are you having your coffee on the back deck?"

"Am I that obvious? Anyway, I'm going to finish my coffee and go for a run. Have a good class, sweetheart. Love you."

"Love you too, Mom," Lauren replied with a sigh.

After she hung up, Lily stood on the back deck in a pair of sweatpants and a hoodie. She held the mug to her lips and watched the sun climb up slowly, bathing the world in warm hues of red and orange. Once it settled in between the clouds, Lily smiled and finished the rest of her drink. Then she went back inside, rinsed her mug, and set it out to dry.

She hummed all the way up the stairs and paused in the doorway to her room. After a quick glance around, she settled on a pair of shorts and a sleeveless top. Then she placed her earphones in, slipped her phone, keys, and wallet into her pockets, and took the stairs two at a time.

At the bottom, she stopped to trace the picture of Mother, a ritual she'd gotten used to since arriving there, and pressed a kiss to the center.

During her run, she couldn't stop thinking about her mother or the circumstances leading to her return to Provincetown. It was hard to imagine her mother in Provincetown at eighteen, the oldest of the Wilson kids, headstrong, opinionated, butting heads with her mother. Yet, the more she learned about her mother's past, including her tumultuous relationship with her father before she left for the city with Eric, the more her heart broke for Kelly.

At eighteen, she'd made the mistake of falling in love with the wrong man, a man who, on paper, at least, had all of the appearance of a knight in shining armor. Everything from coming from a wealthy family to his own wealth and good looks, it was no wonder her mother had fallen head over heels and never looked back.

Lily couldn't imagine what it must've been like to start over in the city, where her mother hadn't known anyone, and to get pregnant at twenty-one, a few short years after running away with the man of her dreams, must've been difficult. Knowing her mother's relationship with her mother had only gone downhill from there only made the knowledge harder to carry.

By the time Lily circled back to the house, she was covered in sweat and still mulling over her mother's past and how lonely and isolating it must've felt. With a slight shake of her head, she made her way into the house and hurried up the stairs. In the shower, she scrubbed every inch of her skin twice before coming out and changing into a fresh set of clothes.

On her way out the door to meet up with a client at

Sabrina's wellness center, Lily's phone rang. She paused with one foot in the air and rummaged through her purse. Without looking at the call log, she pressed the phone to her ear and reached for the other shoe.

"Hey, is this a bad time?"

Lily switched the phone to her other ear. "Hey, Sylvie. I was on my way out. Is everything okay? Are Stan and the kids okay?"

"Yeah, everyone is fine," Sylvie replied, the sound of clattering against the keyboard loud and intrusive. "How are things with you?"

"Everything's fine."

Sylvie stopped typing and exhaled. "I miss you. New York isn't the same without you."

"I miss you too. You, Lucas, and your families should come down and visit me. You'd love it here."

"We'd love that. So, listen, this isn't just a social call. I mean, it is good to hear your voice, but it's not why I called you."

Lily stood up straighter and brushed lint off of her collar. "Okay, what's up?"

"Dad's still upset about what happened during Aunt Mae's funeral. He keeps talking about how out of control you are and how you need to be taught a lesson."

Lily's stomach dipped. "Is he taking it out on Amy?"

Sylvie hesitated. "Mom is...as well as can be expected. You know what it's like for them."

Lily cleared her throat. "Okay."

"I didn't call to tell you about his bouts of anger, or not just that, at least. He's been talking a lot about you when he gets drunk and going off on rants and stuff. The other day, I heard him say something about you and

Lance, how well-matched you were, and how you should be thanking him for what he did."

Ice settled in Lily's stomach and unfurled into something low and heavy. "What are you saying?"

Sylvie sighed. "Look, I don't want to make things worse, but it sounds like he might've been the one to set you up with Lance to stop you from pursuing a career as a dietician."

Lily's blood began to pound in her ears, and her tongue felt heavy. "What?"

"Yeah, he was congratulating himself on that the other day and how well it would've worked if it hadn't been for your impatience and short-sightedness. I knew he was a control freak, but this is..."

Lily had to swallow several times before she could speak. "Taking it to a whole other level?"

"Yeah. I'm sorry. I thought you had the right to know."

"Thank you. Look, I've got to go because I'm meeting up with a client. We'll talk soon, okay?"

"Talk to you soon. Bye."

"Bye."

As soon as Sylvie hung up, Lily leaned against the door and squeezed her eyes shut. Learning Eric had kept her from her mom was one thing. Realizing he had been trying to manipulate her like a puppet in every single aspect of her life, from her career to her marriage, was another.

Lily clenched her hands into fists as red-hot anger burned through her.

It stayed with her as she walked over to Sabrina's spa and into her office. There, she met with a client, a tall redhead with streaks of silver in her hair, and discussed the details of her detox plan. Yet, the entire time, she

161

couldn't shake the thought off, and she kept seeing her father and Lance during all those late-night talks and all the cigars smoked on the terrace.

Had her marriage been a lie too?

A few hours later, she left the wellness center. Lily had no idea what to do and ended up wandering the city streets until she stopped outside of her aunt Heather's house. As soon as she glanced up and caught her aunt's silhouette in the top window, she smiled. Then she fished her phone out of her pocket and called her. Aunt Heather threw the door open, revealing herself in a silk robe and a towel wrapped around her head.

"This is a nice surprise. Come in."

"Sorry to stop by unannounced. Is this a good time?"

"It's always a good time for you, honey. What's on your mind?"

"Can we go for a walk and talk?"

Aunt Heather nodded and removed the towel from the top of her head, revealing wisps of white in her dark hair. "Sure, sweetheart. We can take a walk down to the Beech Forest Trail boardwalk. Let me just change into something more appropriate. Why don't you come in and wait?"

"I can wait out here. I don't mind."

Aunt Heather gave her a confused look and left the door open. She disappeared down the hallway, and the door to her room clicked shut. When Aunt Heather returned in a pair of neon-colored sweatpants and a bright-colored shirt, her hair had been woven into a braid, and she sported a smile. She looped her arm through Lily's, and they fell into step, making their way down to the boardwalk, where the calm blue waters lapped on either side.

"Is Ed in the office today?"

Aunt Heather snorted. "My husband is always in the office. It feels like he's not going to retire until he's dragged out of there."

"He'll slow down eventually, I'm sure," Lily offered after a brief pause. "How are Luke and Tammy?"

"Tammy is thinking of switching to another real estate company, but she's not so sure if it's a good idea. Luke seems to be happy where he is, so that's something at least."

"Uh-huh."

"Okay, what's on your mind? You know I'm not just spunk and fire and good looks. Your aunt's got a good head on her shoulders too, and I know when something is wrong."

Lily sighed when they came to a stop at the railing and glanced out at the distance. "Sylvie called before I left for the wellness center. She told me she thinks my father introduced me to Lance to keep me from being a dietician."

Aunt Heather frowned. "I can't pretend to understand your father, but you know what I do know?"

"Hmm?"

"Kelly and I spent so much time dreaming about the day the two of you would be reunited. She loved you so much, and so do I. I don't know if it helps to know this, but I just want you to know you're not alone."

Lily withdrew her hand and rubbed her bare arm. "How can you be so...calm about what he did?"

"I'm not. Eric took something from us that we'll never be able to get back, and he kept a mother from her child. Kelly was devastated. We all were. It was really hard on Mom and Dad too, knowing you'd grow up without them

163

seeing it or knowing you. However, I also know that it's not going to help to spend time dwelling on what could've been. I'm just grateful to have you here."

Lily gave her aunt a watery smile. "I'm glad to be here too. You have no idea how much. Provincetown turned out to be so much more than what I needed."

A fierce wind ripped past them, and Aunt Heather inched closer and draped an arm over Lily's shoulders. Together, they looked out over the water, glistening underneath the light of the afternoon sun.

Lily inhaled and let her hands fall to her sides. "I want to ask you something."

"Mm-hmm."

"What do you know about Ben?"

Aunt Heather tilted her head to look at her. "Ben Vasquez? The caretaker at the inn?"

Lily nodded and didn't hold her gaze. "Yeah, I know he's been through a tough time, and I wondered if you knew anything else."

"He doesn't talk much about his ex."

"Has he said anything about his daughter?"

Aunt Heather's lips lifted into a smile. "Ah, I see what this is about. You like him."

Lily blushed. "No, I just... He's been really nice to me and helpful, so I wanted to see if there was anything I could do to help him out."

Aunt Heather squeezed her shoulders. "Uh-huh. Well, I know you don't like him and all, but if you did, I would tell you that you should definitely spend more time with him. He's a good person, and I can tell he's a good influence."

Lily's lips twitched. "I'll keep that in mind. So, when were you going to tell me you were in a band?"

"Honey, you didn't think this style just happened, did you? I've been marching to the beat of my own drum since I was sixteen. Oh, the stories I could tell you."

"Like what?"

Aunt Heather chuckled. "I snuck into an Elvis Presley concert once. He told me I was pretty, and we danced together. I'm pretty sure I have a picture somewhere."

"*This* I have to see. I can't believe you got to meet the King of Rock and Roll."

Aunt Heather patted her hand. "Your aunt's led a pretty good life. You play your cards right, and you might do the same. There's still time."

Chapter Nineteen

Lily's hand reached out, blindly groping for her phone. She pushed her hair out of her eyes, pressed it to her ear, and cleared her throat. "Hello?"

"Good morning. I thought you'd be up by now."

Lily yawned and sat up straighter. "I had a late night last night. How are you, sweetheart?"

"I'm fine, Mom. Really looking forward to our trip. I'm sorry Jake couldn't make it."

Lily pried one eye open, her vision swimming in and out of focus. "Hopefully, next time."

"So, about this trip, I was thinking maybe we could have a costume party."

Lily swung her legs over the side of the bed and stumbled into the bathroom. There, she squinted at the particles of light dancing on tile floors and the sound of birds chirping in the distance. Carefully, she set her phone down on the shelf above the sink and set it on speaker. Sara's voice filled the room as Lily cupped her hands underneath the faucet and splashed her face.

With a shiver, she patted her face dry and reached for her toothbrush.

When she spat out a mouthful of toothpaste and rinsed, the doorbell rang. Lily snatched her phone off the shelf, cradled it between her neck and shoulder, and hurried down the stairs. At the bottom of the stairs, she paused to gather her hair into a bun on top of her head. She caught a glimpse of her confused face in the mirror above the shoe rack in the hallway before she twisted the knob.

Her mouth fell open as she glanced between Liam and Sara, both of them wearing pleased expressions. Her phone slid down, and she caught it at the last second. With a beam, she drew them both in for a hug and inhaled the familiar, sweet smell of them. Like lemon-scented soap.

"What are you two doing here? I thought you were coming tomorrow."

Liam pulled back and offered her a bright smile. "We both decided to come down early. Lauren had some work to finish before the big weekend, so she couldn't come."

Lily's gaze kept switching back and forth between the two. "It's so good to see you both. I can't believe you're finally here."

Sara took off her glasses and placed them on top of her head. Her brown eyes were wide and full of humor, her wavy auburn hair was secured in a braid, and her short-clad legs were already covered in sweat. Lily gave her another hug and ushered them both inside, leaving their bags by the door.

Sara let out a low whistle. "You were right. Such a beautiful view. Now I get why you talk about it all the time."

Lily laughed and patted Liam's hand. "I don't talk about it all the time."

Sara draped an arm over her shoulders and squeezed. "When can we go on a tour?"

Liam rolled his eyes. "We got her out of bed. At least give her a chance to have breakfast and change."

"Why don't you two freshen up, and I'll take you out to the beach?"

Sara and Liam exchanged a quick look and nodded. Then Lily led them up the stairs and showed them the rooms that used to belong to her aunts. Sara took the room closer to her, and Lily left her, unzipping her bag and messaging. Liam, on the other hand, took one look around his room, with its pastel-colored walls and small dresser, and frowned.

Lily lingered in the doorway. "You can have one of the rooms downstairs if you'd prefer. I know these are a bit girly."

Liam set his bag down on the bed and unzipped it. "Don't worry, Mom. This is fine. I was just thinking Lauren should've been here. I'm not sure if she's going to be able to come down or not."

"I know. It'll be okay, honey. Tough times don't last."

"Tough people do?"

Lily nodded. "I'll let you get settled. See you downstairs."

With one final smile, she darted down the carpeted hallway to her own room, and the door clicked shut behind her. In the bathroom, she raced through her morning routine, impatient to scrub herself in the shower and apply her facial creams. When she came back out, she dragged a brush through her hair and pulled on a short-sleeved, knee-length floral dress.

Downstairs, Sara and Liam already stood, dressed identically in shorts and T-shirts and studying the pictures on the walls. As soon as they looked up at her, a surge of gratitude and disbelief washed over her, and it left her in awe all over again.

Lily couldn't believe how lucky she was to have them.

She draped one arm on either side of them and led them outside through the sliding glass door and onto the grounds. With a smile, she led them down the gentle slope along the dunes and paused to gesture at the house, glistening underneath the early morning sun.

Lily kept up a steady stream of conversation, filling them in on the town's history as they picked their way through the path leading directly onto the beach. There, she came to a stop at the edge of the water and lifted her gaze up to the sun. Out of the corner of her eye, she saw her children do the same, awe and pleasure etched onto their faces.

Sara took out her phone and snapped a few pictures of them.

"So, when are we going to meet everyone?" Liam straightened his back and glanced away from the water. "Or are we too early?"

Lily chuckled and squeezed his hand. "The inn is open today, so we can go meet up with your great-aunts Heather and Rebecca. Not sure if Angie will be in this early, but we should run into her too."

Sara quickened her pace to catch up to Lily. "Angie is Aunt Rebecca's daughter, right? She's the chef?"

Lily nodded. "You'll love her food. I don't know what she uses, but it's amazing."

"Who's she married to again?" Liam asked, pausing to shove his hands into the pockets of his shorts. "I couldn't make heads or tails of your family tree sheet, by the way. No offense, Mom."

"It'll take some time, but you'll get used to it," Lily assured him with a quick smile. "Angie isn't married, and she doesn't have any children. She works at the Herring Cove Restaurant attached to the Herring Cove Inn, along with her mother."

Liam nodded and caught up to her easily. "Good to know."

In silence, the three of them walked back to the main house and explored. Sara paused to admire the white clapboard siding, the navy-blue shutters, and the sloping, gabled roofline. Then, the three of them fell into an easy rhythm as they wandered through the sunny streets of Provincetown, with Lily pausing to greet a few people by name.

The sun was high in the sky, set against a backdrop of clear blue skies, when Lily came to a stop outside the Herring Cove Inn, bathed in warm, buttery hues. She pushed the door open and immediately spotted her aunt Rebecca in a colorful pair of pants, a billowing blouse, and a single streak of silver in her brown hair. Aunt Rebecca said something to Alice in a low tone before she spun around, her eyes widening in surprise.

Her mouth formed a surprised 'O,' and her hands fell to her sides.

All at once, she hurried over and drew Liam and Sara in for a long, extended hug, during which she fussed over them and sniffed. By the time she drew back, her face was flushed, and her eyes were filled with tears. She glanced between the two of them and paused to clear her throat.

"I can't believe we're finally doing this," Aunt

Rebecca exclaimed, her voice ringing through the empty reception. "Heather, you need to get out here right now."

"I thought you wanted my help with..." Aunt Heather trailed off as she spotted the three of them and did a double take.

She took long, measured strides and drew Sara and Liam in for another hug, with the three of them spinning in a circle before they settled. Lily used the back of her hand to dash away the tears.

She couldn't believe it was finally happening. All she needed in that moment was Lauren, and her happiness would be complete.

Aunt Heather was openly crying, her weathered face creasing as she glanced around. She paused to pull a pack of tissues out of her dress and blew her nose loudly. Then she and Aunt Rebecca were talking over each other, their voices rising in excitement as they tugged on her children.

Once they stepped through the double doors of the kitchen, a blast of steam hit Lily in the face. She greeted Angie, who hugged each of her kids warmly before returning to the stove and the hissing sound it was making. Everyone in the kitchen called out to them in earnest before lapsing into silence, the sounds of pots and pans filling the air.

Aunt Heather led them all into the café, where she commanded a table by the window and pulled a few chairs out. "What can we get you guys to eat? I can have the kitchen whip up something special."

Sara smiled. "Oh, that's okay. We had breakfast on the road."

Aunt Rebecca waved her comment away. "Nonsense. You haven't lived till you've tried the food around here.

I'll have Angie whip up something special. Either of you have any allergies?"

"You don't have to go through all of that trouble, ma'am. I'm sure we can—"

Aunt Rebecca fixed her brown eyes on Liam and raised an eyebrow. "Don't sass me, boy. There aren't any ma'ams around here. It's Aunt Rebecca to you."

Liam flushed and lowered himself onto his chair. "Okay."

"Ben." Aunt Heather spotted him on the other side of the restaurant, screwdriver in one hand and a hammer in the other. "Come over here and meet Lily's kids."

Lily blushed. "Aunt Heather, I'm sure he's got work to do. Don't bother him."

Ben walked over to them, his dark locks matted to his forehead and in tufts on top of his head, and his lips spreading into a slow, welcoming smile. "It's nice to meet both of you. Lily has told us all so much about you."

"Nice to meet you," they both echoed after a quick look in their mother's direction.

Lily studiously avoided their gaze and took a seat at the head of the table, offering her a view of the quiet side street and the sparkling waters beyond. After some biscuits and iced lemonade, during which her aunts fussed over her children and hung on to their every word, Lily ushered them out of the café and onto the busy street.

A short while later, the three of them sat down at a restaurant overlooking the Provincetown harbor, and Lily leaned back to look at them, the swell of emotion in her chest only growing stronger.

"Betsy's Bayside restaurant is beautiful," Sara

commented with a quick look around the warm, earthy colors and the wooden tables lined up on either side of the walls. "The whole island is beautiful."

"I think I can see why you love it here," Liam added with a smile. "It's definitely got something."

Over a lunch of clam chowder, lobster rolls, and burgers, the three of them talked and laughed, falling back into old habits quickly. After lunch, they took another walk along the beach, the conversation turning more serious and subdued as she listened to each of them talk about work, school, and their respective partners.

Lily's mouth hurt from smiling as they walked back to the house.

There, she dimmed the lights and lit a few candles. Liam made some popcorn and filled up bowls with chips. Sara brought out a bottle of wine and a pitcher of iced lemonade. By the dim light of the candles, the three of them sat around crossed-legged on the carpet and told stories.

Hours later, Lily's head was still buzzing as she scrolled through the movie selection and settled on one. Liam commandeered one of the couches and brought his arms up over his head. Lily paused to drape a blanket over him and press a kiss to his forehead. Sara, on the other hand, took the other couch and curled up against it, a handful of popcorn in one hand and a glass of wine in the other.

By the time the end credits came, both of her children were fast asleep, with Liam's soft snores filling the room. She glanced over at Sara, curled into a ball with her mouth half open, and smiled. When she flipped onto her back, Lily could almost believe they were still in their penthouse in New York, enjoying another quiet movie night while Lance worked.

Once she squeezed her eyes shut, the familiar smell of popcorn and chips wafting around her, she could almost tell herself nothing had changed at all.

Chapter Twenty

Lily held her breath as she paused to lace up her shoes. Once she was done, she tied a sweater around her waist and pocketed her keys. Then she tiptoed, frowning at the creaking sound the floorboards made. When she pulled the glass door shut behind her, she breathed a sigh of relief. With Sara and Liam still deep in the throes of sleep in her living room, she wanted to go for a quick run.

She set off at a brusque pace, mentally going over her to-do list for the day.

At noon, Lauren was due to arrive, followed closely by her grandparents, Stu, Ian, and Sophia. In a few short hours, her house was going to be filled to the brim with family, with many of them staying in the inn, a few at her aunt's, and one or two in her own house in the spare rooms downstairs.

Lily's stomach was full of butterflies.

She couldn't imagine what it was going to be like to have so many family members under one roof. With a smile, she made her way back to the house and snuck back in through the front door. In the shower, she took her time with the loofah, running it over her skin until steam filled the bathroom and her peach-scented shower gel filled the room.

When she came out, she changed into a knee-length dress and made her way downstairs. After securing her earphones, she mouthed along to the music and set down flour, eggs, and bacon on the counter. A short while later, Sara stumbled into the kitchen in a daze and poured herself a cup of coffee. Through sleep-filled eyes, she gave her mother a one-armed hug and a grunt.

Liam gulped down an entire cup of coffee before acknowledging either of them. With a chuckle, Lily set out a pan full of scrambled eggs, crispy bacon, a stack of pancakes, and freshly squeezed orange juice. Sara had juice dribbling down her chin, and Liam's mouth was stuffed with food when Lauren arrived, bright-eyed and wearing a knee-length blue dress with brown hair piled on top of her head.

She gave her mom a quick hug and glanced over at her siblings. "What's up with you two? Crawl out of a cave?"

Sara gave her a dark look and grunted.

Liam swallowed and took a long sip of his drink. "We missed you last night, sis. Movie night wasn't the same."

Lauren threw an eggshell at him. "I can't believe you had movie night without me."

Lily draped an arm over Lauren's shoulders and squeezed. "We can do another movie night tonight, sweetheart. How was your schoolwork? Did you get everything done?"

Lauren nodded and set down her purse. "Yeah, I

think I'm actually ahead, which is good because there's a lot of heavy courses this semester."

Sara set her drink down, some of it sloshing over. "You're such a showoff."

Lauren stuck her tongue out at her. "Oh, whatever. You're just jealous."

Liam pushed his chair back with a screech. "It is too early in the day for this. Mom, can't you make them stop?"

"It's half past twelve in the afternoon," Lily replied, pausing to take the plate from Liam. "We've got a lot to do around the house. Lauren, why don't you freshen up and have something to eat while Sara and Liam help me in the backyard?"

Lauren nodded and pushed herself off the counter. "I'm sharing a room with Sara, right?"

"It's the door in the middle," Sara replied, pausing to stand up. "And I already claimed the bed by the window, so don't even think about ignoring the rules of dibs."

Lauren scowled and muttered something under her breath.

After they changed out of their clothes and washed their faces, Liam and Sara followed her into the small backyard underneath the back porch with a short, white picket fence. In silence, they spread out the picnic tables along with their tablecloths. Once they were done, the three of them set up their games, including a life-size Jenga, ladder ball, and beanbags for the toss. Lauren materialized toward the end and helped them move everything around to tie the look in.

Then they all went in and helped Lily set up the last of the streamers and balloons. When they finished, Lily stepped back to admire their handiwork and placed both hands on her hips.

"This looks amazing. You guys did a great job."

"You did most of the hard work, Mom," Lauren praised, giving her a warm smile. "Liam and Sara are going to show me around town. Do you want to come with?"

Lily shook her head. "I'm going to clean up for a bit and make sure everything is in order for tomorrow."

"We can stay and help," Sara offered with a quick look around the room. "There isn't much to do."

Lily waved their comment away. "Don't be silly, sweetheart. The three of you deserve to go out and have fun. I'm going to finish up here, and I might go for a walk."

In spite of their protests, Lily pushed them out the door. Then she rolled up the sleeves of her dress and put away the dishes. After the last of the food was put away and the entire place looked presentable after supper, she changed into a pair of sweatpants and a hoodie.

Outside, the evening air was warm and balmy, and a crescent-shaped moon hung in the middle of the sky. She tucked away her phone and her keys and exited around the back. In the distance, she heard the waves crash against the shore and inhaled, wanting to savor the moment. When she released her breath, it echoed back to her in the stillness.

Lily was lost in thought, reliving what it felt like to have all three children under one roof again, when the sound of raised voices reached her. She squinted into the distance, the lamps barely helping her to distinguish two silhouettes walking straight toward her. She stopped along the edge of the water and shoved both hands into her pockets. When they got closer, she saw the woman first, petite and with red hair and clear hazel eyes.

Then she recognized Ben, his dark brown hair tousled to the side and an unfamiliar tightness around his hazel eyes. He straightened when he saw her, and some of the tension in his shoulders melted. Once they were close enough, Lily recognized the woman with him as his sister, Olive.

Almost as soon as she recognized her, Lily remembered her tragic backstory.

Ben's smile made his whole face light up, and it filled her stomach with butterflies. "Looking for treasure?"

Lily smiled. "You got me. I'm not having much luck though."

"You might want to look farther out," Ben suggested with a small smile. "Or hire treasure hunters."

"And have to split the profit? No way."

Ben's smile grew bigger. "Lily, this is my sister, Olive. Olive, this is Lily Alrich. She's Rebecca and Heather's niece."

"The prodigal niece finds her way back." Olive held her hand out and gave Lily a quick shake. "You're pretty famous around here. I hope you know that isn't going to die down anytime soon."

Lily withdrew her hand and nodded. "I figured as much, at least until the next interesting thing."

"I might have you beat there," Ben joked, pausing to run a hand over his face. "Grace, my daughter, is going to be visiting, and whenever she's in town, people tend to talk about me."

Lily's heart soared. "You reached out to her? Oh, Ben, that's great news. I hope it goes well."

A shadow settled over Ben's face. "I haven't reached

out to her yet. I'm not even sure why. Every time I think of picking up the phone, I just...don't have the words."

Olive cleared her throat, face half shrouded in darkness. "She's coming to visit me."

"And she won't even tell me when or where they're going to meet up," Ben muttered with a frustrated glance in his sister's direction. "How's that for betrayal?"

Olive blew out a breath and shifted from one foot to the other. "We talked about this already, Ben. She asked me not to tell you. I can't betray her trust like that."

Ben threw his arms up on either side of him and muttered something unflattering under his breath. He picked up a pebble, drifted away, and tossed it into the water. Lily watched him for a few seconds before she realized Olive was studying her openly and without apology.

"I've heard a lot about you from Ben."

Lily's lips lifted into a half smile. "Good things, I hope."

Olive nodded. "I think you could be good for Ben if he wasn't being an idiot. Ben's been hurt before, so he doesn't like to open up to people. It's hard for him."

"I understand."

Olive stepped closer, her hazel eyes filled with some strange emotion. "At the risk of sounding like a cliché, don't hurt my brother, okay? He deserves better."

"Your brother and I are just friends."

Olive raised an eyebrow. "I've seen the way you look at him, and with the way he talks about you...yeah, I'm not buying that. It's none of my business, anyway. I'm just giving you my two cents."

Silence stretched between them.

"Are you really not going to tell him when she's going to come visit?"

"Would you?"

Lily sighed. "No, I guess not. It's not an easy situation to be in, but I know he really wants to reconnect with her."

Olive glanced over at her brother, her expression turning sad. "And he will, but she has to be eased into it. He can't just snap his fingers and have everything go right."

"I understand."

Olive switched her gaze back to Lily, and her expression softened. "I had a feeling you would, based on everything I've heard about you."

The two of them lapsed into another pregnant silence.

Ben materialized by their sides, his expression giving nothing away. "We should get going, Olive. It's late."

"It was nice to meet you, Lily. I hope we get to spend more time together soon."

"Me too," Lily murmured, with a quick glance in Ben's direction. She stood up straighter and linked her fingers behind her back. "I know this is short notice, and you two probably already have plans, but on the off chance you don't, I'm throwing a party tomorrow for Memorial Day; you two should come."

Ben's expression turned surprised. "I thought that was for family only."

Lily gave him a confused look. "No, it's not. You're both welcome to come. We'd love to have you."

At least it would take Ben's mind off his daughter's situation because Lily had no idea how else she was meant to help him.

"We'll try to make it," Olive offered with a small smile. "Thanks for the invite, Lily. Good night."

"Good night."

Lily watched them retreat back down the beach. She waited until they were specks in the darkness before she spun around and made her way back up the path and to her house. She didn't even realize that her heart was racing or her palms were sweating until she leaned against the glass door and smiled.

Ben Vasquez tended to have that effect on her, much to her surprise.

Chapter Twenty-One

L ily untied her apron, tossed it onto the counter, and threw the door open. Aunt Ashley, her husband, and her kids stood on her front porch in shorts and T-shirts, her aunt's hair piled on top of her head, a few wisps of silver glistening underneath the sun. After giving her and her husband, Jude, a quick hug, she turned to Aunt Ashley's kids, her cousins, Jeff, Emily, and Tara, and lingered during their group hug.

Then she was welcoming Jeff's wife, Tay, and their two kids, Jason and Maria, who were the spitting image of their parents with their dark hair and short stature. Another car pulled up next to the curb, and Emily's kids, Charlotte and Savannah, came out, sporting sun-kissed skin and bright smiles. Tara's daughter, Ruby, trailed after them, tugging on the sleeves of her long sweatshirt, and her hands moved to the pink highlights in her hair.

Lily was on the back porch, introducing her aunt Ashley's family to her kids and marveling at the warmth and laughter radiating from everyone when Aunt Rebecca's kids arrived. Rob had his arms around his wife, Alice, the two of them exchanging loving glances as they handed Lily a container full of food. Terry hurried in, red-faced and marching her kids, Lara and Glen Jr., in tow. Angie, who had been in the kitchen for the past three hours, helping Lily set everything up, came out to greet them, her blond hair matted to her forehead and her brown eyes filled with humor.

Sara, Liam, and Lauren settled in for a game of Jenga with her cousins.

Cheers and laughter rose through the air.

Her aunts sat on the back deck, playing cards and nibbling on some of the appetizers. Lily was setting down a few more trays of food and wiping her hands on her apron when the doorbell rang, bringing her back to the present with a jolt. With a smile, Lily opened the door to reveal her uncle Frankie's weathered face, his thinning hair tucked underneath a cap. His wife, Paula, drew her in for a hug before motioning to their children, Jonathan and Suzie.

Jonathan and Suzie took a few more games out of the trunk and waved over at her. In the doorway, Jonathan introduced her to his wife, Joanne, and his two children, Jaxson and Reese, a pair of sullen-looking teenagers, who barely glanced up from their phones when they were introduced. It wasn't long before the two of them found Terry's kids, Laura and Glen Jr., and the four of them made their way to the beach for a quick swim.

Lily paused to lean against the railing and look out at them.

Down below, her uncle Frankie was already starting on the barbecue, hot steam wafting through the air as he fanned himself. Her aunt Heather's kids, Tammy and

Luke, stood on either side of him, sipping on their iced lemonade and making small talk.

Conversation rose and fell around her as Lily hurried in and out of the kitchen.

By the time plates of food were being set out, the smell of spices and grilled seafood lingering in the air, her grandparents arrived with Ian, Sophia, and Stu in tow. Grandma Jen and Grandpa Frank pulled her in for a long hug, and Lily held on to them for a long time, the familiar swell in her chest growing.

She gave her siblings long hugs and smiled at Ian's kids, Kelly, Dana, and Dean.

Ian's wife, Lucy, wandered through the house, marveling at the architecture, with Sophia in tow. Sophia's two kids, Zac and Zoe, were the last to arrive, sporting apologetic expressions and carrying more bags filled with food and games. When Sophia's ex emerged on Lily's doorstep, she kept an eye on her sister out of the corner of her eye.

Sophia and Darren exchanged a quick hug before he came in.

He nodded in Lily's general direction when they were introduced and didn't say anything. Everyone else greeted him by name as he stepped out onto the back porch and vanished in the crowd of people gathered. Lily returned to the kitchen, glanced around at the trays of food on the counter, and draped an arm over her stomach.

"I have no idea how we're pulling it off, but we are," Lily told Angie with a quick shake of her head. "I couldn't have done any of this without you."

Lara, Glen Jr., Jaxson, and Reese raced past a short while later, all of them drenched in sweat. The doors to the guest rooms slammed shut, and Lily twisted to face Angie, her brows furrowed together.

"Should we check on them?"

Angie bent down in front of a tray of crab sandwiches and drew her bottom lip between her teeth. "The boys tend to go overboard with the roughhousing. I wouldn't worry about it just yet."

"When should I worry?"

Laughter continued to rise through the air.

"I don't know. Maybe if one of them tries to kill the other," Angie suggested without looking at her. "You've got kids. You know how it is."

"Ever thought of having any of your own?"

Angie stood up and used the back of her hand to wipe the sweat off her brow. "Sometimes, I think about it, but I haven't met the right man, and call me old-fashioned, but I want to have it all, you know?"

Lily sighed. "I know."

"Hey, Ang." Suzie came in, ruffled her cousin's hair, and sniffed. "This smells amazing. By the way, I can't believe we're just getting the chance to meet, Lily. I've already heard so much about you."

"Likewise."

Angie batted Suzie's hand away and gave her a dirty look. "Get out. Every time you're in the kitchen, you end up inhaling my food."

Suzie gave her a wounded look. "It's not my fault your food is delicious."

"I banned you and Jonathan from the kitchen for a reason."

"She's the one who ate the crab cakes," Jonathan protested from the back porch. He wandered over to them, and his eyes immediately went to the lobster rolls. "I could help you carry stuff out."

Angie snorted. "The last time you tried to help me carry stuff, half of the food went missing."

Jonathan frowned. "Come on, cous. Where's the trust?"

"There's none. Don't make me call Grandma Jen. She'll give you all her famous look, and you'll wish you hadn't bothered me."

With a laugh, Suzie and Jonathan joined the aunts on the back porch. Lily was organizing more of the fries onto trays when Stu came into the kitchen in a Hawaiian shirt and shorts, his blond hair slicked back. He offered Lily a warm smile as he poured himself some lemonade.

"You know, your mom had a knack for making people feel welcome too," Stu said in between sips of his drink. "You look so much like her right now."

Lily wiped her hands on the back of her jeans to hide the tremor in them. "Thank you."

She wasn't ready for Stu to see that side of her yet, not when she still had so much to unpack about her mother.

"Next time you're in town, we should get some lunch or something. I'll show you some of her favorite spots and tell you some stories."

Lily's heart missed a beat. "I'd really like that."

When he left, Lily released a deep breath and twisted to face Angie. "I'm glad it's not weird for him because of, you know, my father."

Angie shook her head. "Stu never cared your mom was married before. He only cared that your dad didn't treat her well, and he's actually always wanted to meet you."

Lily offered Angie a tight smile and said nothing.

No matter how good of a man Stu was, none of this could've been easy for him. While she knew he had nothing against her personally, having her there, the daughter of the man who made Kelly's life miserable, must've been a difficult reminder.

When he looked at her, did he really see Kelly, or could he only see everything that was taken from him? Was Stu able to separate her from her father's actions?

Jeff, Emily, and Tara came in a short while later while Lily was mulling over the idea and arranging the dining table. All three siblings talked over each other and joked with Lily, regaling her with stories of their childhood in Falmouth. Then Ruby came in, and Angie beckoned her into the kitchen, where the teenager with large, sad eyes helped set up trays of food.

Lily kept sneaking glances at her and wondering if she was okay.

Out of the corner of her eye, she spotted her own kids deep in the throes of a heated game of beanbag toss. Lauren, Sara, and Sophia were in stitches while Ian and Liam scowled in their general direction. Then, more food was being brought out, and Uncle Frankie came in with trays of barbecued meat and chicken. He stopped to pat his belly, earning an eye roll from Paula. As everyone was sitting down, the doorbell rang again, revealing an eager Olive in a pink strapless dress, carrying a tray of lasagna, and a less eager-looking Ben, who had a thin sheen of sweat on his forehead and carried two packs of beer. Wordlessly, he set them down on the table and offered Lily a smile, looking handsome in his dark jeans and shirt.

He and Lily barely exchanged more than a few words before he and Olive were whisked outside and swallowed whole by the Wilson clan. Lily's feet ached as she instructed Kelly, Dean, and Dana on how to set the last of the tables. Zac and Zoe carried out the last of the drinks and called out to everyone. Then plates of food were being passed around, and Lily collapsed into the nearest chair at the head of the dining table, discreetly rubbing the soles of her feet underneath it.

Her grandparents and children embraced again before taking their seats near her, talking at a million miles a minute. Lily's eyes filled with tears as she glanced around, unable to believe how she had gotten here or the fact she could've had this all along.

Grandma Jen set down her napkin and patted Lily's hand. "What's on your mind, sweetheart?"

"I just can't stop thinking about the fact I could've had this sooner. If Dad hadn't...if he hadn't kept me away from you guys. I've lost so much time."

She thought of the matter with equal amounts of disgust at her father's behavior and heartache over what could've been.

Lily had no idea how she was meant to forgive him for this. Or if she even could.

She ran a hand over her face. "I've been trying to find a way to forgive him and make my peace with all of this, but I don't know how."

Grandpa Frank covered her hand with his. "You give yourself some time, honey. There's no reason to have it all figured out right now."

"Yeah?"

Grandma Jen nodded and squeezed her shoulders. "Absolutely, you take all the time you need."

By the end of the meal, when everyone was sprawled over the couches in her living room and on the back deck, patting their bellies and smiling, her grandparents stood up together and held up their glasses.

"Lily, you have no idea how happy we are to finally have you here," Grandma Jen began with a quick look around the room. "I don't know if you can feel how much love we have for you, how much love we've always had for you."

Lily's eyes filled with tears.

She tried and failed to find the words to express exactly how she felt at that moment, but she knew nothing was ever going to be sufficient. There weren't enough words in the whole of the English language to describe how she felt about being included—about them wanting her to have a home with them.

"I remember how much your mother loved this beach house," Grandma Jen continued in a quieter voice. "Our darling Kelly would've loved this. She really looked forward to sharing this house with you."

Tears trickled down Lily's cheeks.

She could picture her mother as the young and carefree woman she once was, full of life and enthusiasm, full of exuberance and hope for the future. Suddenly, it was almost as if Kelly was there, watching over all of them with a smile.

I hope you've found peace, Mom. You deserve it.

"When Kelly came back to us, we were overjoyed," Grandpa Frank continued, his voice catching toward the end. "As many of you know, we did not leave things on the best of terms when she left for the city with Eric, but we never stopped loving her or wishing the best for her."

A quiet murmur rose through the room.

Grandma Jen dabbed her eyes with a handkerchief.

"I'm sorry if we've gone and made this emotional, Lily. This was meant to be a happy occasion."

Lily shook her head and offered them both a watery smile. "I can't think of a better way to celebrate Memorial Day weekend than by honoring my mother with all of you, the people who knew her best."

"To Kelly," Uncle Frank called out. "May her memory always live on, and may we always carry her in our hearts."

Grandma Jen waited until everyone took a sip of their drinks and cleared her throat. "We would've liked to have seen you and Kelly reunited, but I know she's watching over us now, and I'm sure she's happy we're all here."

A few people were crying openly, and Lily's own chest was tight with disbelief and joy.

"Thank you for finding your way back to us." Grandma Jen held her glass up, her eyes glistening with tears. "Having you here, Lily, has been like having a part of my dear Kelly back. You can't imagine how much it means to me. How much it means to all of us."

"I love you, Grandma," Lily told her in between her tears. She glanced away from her grandparents and took in her mother's family, all of them looking back at her with love and acceptance. "I never thought I could have a family like this. Thank you for welcoming me."

"You've always been a Wilson," Grandpa Frank told her with a lift of his chin. "You'll always be welcome here."

Grandma Jen gave her another wobbly smile and leaned into her grandpa's side.

Grandpa Frank draped an arm over his wife's shoulders and kissed her cheek. He stood up straighter, his eyes sweeping over the room before they landed on Lily. "We want you to have Herring Cove Beach house. We've wanted you to have it from the moment you reached out, and now that you're here, we hope you'll stay for good."

A cheer rose through the crowd.

Lily's mouth fell open in shock, and another surge of disbelief rose through her. Something low and warm unfurled in the center of her stomach, and it took tears building in the corners of her eyes for Lily to recognize the swell of emotion as a mixture of joy and peace. Although she hadn't expected her grandparents' generous offer, it didn't surprise her as much as she thought it would. A part of her had already come to think of Herring Cove Beach house as her home. It had been since the minute she set foot there, and this was just official.

How had she ended up being so fortunate?

Lily lifted her glass, and it took her a few tries to speak. "I can't think of anything I'd love more. I only wish we'd been in each other's lives sooner. Cheers, everyone. Here's to all of us."

A chorus of well wishes resounded, and Lily couldn't help but think of her mother and how much she would've loved all of this.

Chapter Twenty-Two

"Penny for your thoughts?"

Lily eyed her aunt Ashely over the rim of her coffee mug, getting a brief glimpse of the silver streak in her hair before her aunt sat down and tucked the edges of her shawl around her shoulders. Aunt Ashely turned her weathered face to the railing and studied the water.

"How about two pennies?"

Aunt Ashley laughed. "Worth that much, huh?"

Lily took a long sip of her coffee and set it down on the table between them. "I was just thinking about how well the party went. I used to host them all the time in New York, but I honestly can't remember the last time I had this much fun."

Aunt Ashley's hand darted out, her brown eyes full of warmth. "I'm so happy you decided to stay, and I hope we'll be seeing more of you in Falmouth."

Lily smiled. "I hope so too. You know I would've been happy to host Uncle Jude, Jeff, Emily, and Tara too. We can still make room for them if you want."

Aunt Ashley waved her comment away. "Don't worry, sweetheart. Jude is happy to be staying with his parents. His parents have been on a cruise, and it's been a while since they've had a chance to catch up."

"What about the rest?"

"Jeff and Tay are staying with Tay's family, and their kids are enjoying the chance to get to know that side of the family better. Emily and her daughters are really enjoying the inn, and so are Tara and Ruby. There really is nothing to worry about."

Lily offered her aunt a reassuring smile. "If you change your mind, let me know. I'd be more than happy to have them."

In silence, they both turned to the horizon, watching the waves crash against the shore. The early morning sun was already high in the sky, with only a few clouds drifting on the horizon. When Sara and Lauren emerged in their sweatpants and shirts, wearing sleepy expressions, Lily patted the space next to her.

Sara sat on her right and propped her feet against the table.

Lauren sank lower onto her left and lifted the mug up to her face. "We had so much fun, Mom. I had no idea anyone could have so many relatives. I don't think your family tree sheet is going to cut it anymore."

Aunt Ashely choked back a laugh. "So, that's what that was. I saw a glimpse of it the other day, and I couldn't make heads or tails of it."

"It's Mom's cheat sheet," Sara announced proudly. "It helps her keep track of who's who."

Lily offered her aunt an apologetic smile. "I don't want to offend anyone."

Aunt Ashley chuckled. "Oh, honey. Everyone gets

194

the names mixed up. Even after all these years, I still do. How can you not? You'll get used to it, don't worry."

Lily reached for her mug and took another sip. "I hope you all slept well."

"Like a baby," Sara announced, sinking lower into the couch. "The beds are so comfortable here."

"You were snoring like an old man," Lauren grumbled with a dark look in her sister's direction. "I remember why I don't like sharing a room with you."

"I've got an extra bed in the room downstairs if either of you want to bunk with me," Aunt Ashley offered with a quick look between the two of them. "Honestly, though, I remember sharing a room with my sisters, and I loved every minute."

"You did?"

"Most of the time," Aunt Ashley admitted, pausing to tuck her russet-colored hair behind her ears. "Speaking of family, have you given any more thought to what you want to do about your dad, Lily?"

Lily's stomach twisted into knots. "I talked to Grandma and Grandpa about it yesterday, but I'm still not sure. The last time we spoke, I called him out on it... on all of it, and he said nothing. He just called to give me a piece of his mind about coming out here."

Aunt Ashley sighed. "There's no right or wrong way to handle this, sweetheart."

Lily took another long sip of her coffee and set the mug down. "I want to reach out to him again and give him one more chance to own up to all of this. I know it's not going to change anything, but I need to hear him say it."

A part of her wanted to hear the words from his lips.

Knowing he acknowledged the role he played in keeping her mother away from her was a start. It wasn't going to change what he did or bring back the time she and her mother could've had, but Lily at least wanted to know he was sorry. That he wasn't the same person anymore.

Because the more she learned about her father and the kind of man he truly was, the less she liked him. Everything from the way he treated her mother and the lies he'd told her to the role he'd played in introducing her to her ex-husband, Lance. None of it gave him any redeeming qualities.

But Lily couldn't write him off.

Not yet.

Not without giving him a chance, once and for all, to become the man he should be.

"Grandpa is a proud man," Sara said without looking at her. "Are you sure it'll work?"

"I have no idea if it'll work," Lily admitted. "Either way, I have to try because I can't live like this."

She needed answers, one way or another, to determine what kind of role, if any, her father was going to have in her new life.

Lauren cleared her throat. "We've got your back, either way, Mom. Whatever you decide."

"Breakfast's ready," Liam called out, his voice drifting over to where they sat. "Come and get it."

"Make sure you have the food poisoning medication ready," Lauren joked, pausing to stand up and stretch her arm over her head. "Whose idea was it to have Liam cook anyway?"

"I don't know, but keep your napkin close," Sara murmured with a shake of her head. "Do you remember when he tried to make that turkey for Thanksgiving two years ago? I still have nightmares about that."

"I heard that. Are you guys going to come and eat or what?"

In between fits of laughter, the four of them stepped back into the house and found Liam in the kitchen, an apron tied around his waist and a thin sheen of sweat on his forehead. He used the back of his hand to wipe the sweat off his face and gestured to the counter covered in eggs, bacon, hash browns, and a stack of waffles.

Lily's stomach grumbled at the sight. "Sweetheart, this looks amazing."

Liam pointed a spatula at his sisters and scowled. "For your information, I've been taking cooking classes, and Laura thinks I'm a great cook."

Sara pulled her chair out. "Oh, is that why she didn't come with you? Because she's tired of your cooking?"

"Poor Laura. She's got to spend her entire life stuck with him. Maybe it's not too late for us to take her out of it," Lauren added, pausing to pour herself some orange juice. "It's our duty to warn her."

Liam untied the apron and threw it at his sisters. "You two suck."

"We love you," they chorused.

Liam grumbled something under his breath and piled food onto his plate. "No one is making you eat this food. I know Mom and Aunt Ashley will like the food, won't you?"

Aunt Ashley filled her plate with eggs and some bacon. "I already love it, dear. You've got the makings of a chef."

Liam gave his sisters a triumphant look. "See?"

Sara rolled her eyes. "She just feels sorry for you, doofus."

"And she has to be nice because she's staying with us,"

Lauren added before sticking her tongue out at her brother. "Big bro reeks of desperation."

For the rest of breakfast, they all teased each other and laughed.

After they were finished, all of them helped put away the food and clean up the table. Then, all three of her children left the house to go explore, leaving Lily alone with her aunt Ashley. She raced upstairs to get one of her sweaters, and when she came back down, Aunt Ashley was studying the pictures on the wall, her eyes welling with tears.

Aunt Ashley touched a picture of all of the Wilson siblings with the beach in the background, and her lips lifted into a half smile. "Your mother would've been so proud of you, Lily. I'm sure of it."

Lily tied the sweater around her waist and steered them outside, another pang of yearning for the mother she never knew hitting her. "I wish I could've known her."

"Me too."

In silence, they made their way down to the beach and walked along the edge of the water. Lily wove in and out of the few people who were there, trying to gather her thoughts. Halfway through their walk, she took her phone out of her pocket and steeled herself for the phone call.

It took every ounce of courage she had to dial her father's number and wait.

Aunt Ashely drifted away after a quick pat on the back and a comforting smile. "I'm nearby if you need me."

Her father picked up on the sixth ring, sounding annoyed and preoccupied. "What?"

Lily pressed two fingers to her temples. "Is this what our relationship is going to boil down to now? You can't even be happy to hear from me."

"You made your feelings about me pretty clear during the funeral."

Lily rubbed her fingers in slow, circular motions. "*You're* the one who made it clear that you were disappointed with me, and let's be real, Dad, I'm never going to be good enough, am I?"

Eric muttered something unintelligible.

"I've spent my whole life trying to win your approval by making myself smaller, by letting you walk all over me, but I don't want to do that anymore."

"I wasn't aware that providing you with a good life was such a horrible thing," Eric replied stiffly. "It must've been awful to grow up with all that wealth and privilege and to have every opportunity handed to you."

"It's not all about money and power, Dad. Or even knowing the right people. It's about being happy and surrounding yourself with good people."

"'Good people' like your mother's family who have poisoned you against me?"

"They didn't poison me against you, Dad. You did that all on your own. You made that decision the second you decided to lie to me about Mom. You could've told me the truth."

"I did what I had to do in order to protect you. Kelly was not fit to be a mother."

A lump rose in the back of Lily's throat. "What about Aunt Mae? You lied to me about her too."

"Your aunt Mae was a traitor, choosing to help your mother rather than side with her own brother. She chose her own fate."

"And Lance? Was he chosen as my fate too?"

"Lance was a good match," Eric replied in an even voice. "I will not apologize for setting you up with him.

You were drowning and needed some guidance. He helped steer you in the right direction."

A tear slid down Lily's cheek, and a sense of helplessness washed over her, followed by dismay for the father he never was and would never be. She'd been clinging to a lie by the skin of her teeth, and she had nothing at all to show for it. Only the hollow ache in the center of her chest.

"You're not even sorry at all, are you?"

"A father does what he has to do in order to provide for his children. I gave you a good life, and I did what I had to do. Why would I apologize for that?"

"Because you lied, and you twisted the truth to suit your own narrative," Lily whispered, crying freely now. "I don't want our relationship to be like this, Dad. This isn't how it's supposed to be. But I don't know if I can have someone like you in my life right now."

Lily hadn't realized the line went dead until she pulled the phone away from her ear and saw her tear-stained reflection mirrored back to her. When her kids returned, they found her on the beach, sitting on the sand with her knees drawn up to her chest. In silence, they comforted her as she cried and lamented what she had to do.

Moving forward, there was no more room for her father.

Lily knew she was making the right decision, but it didn't make it hurt any less.

Chapter Twenty-Three

Lily leaned over the railing and paused to tighten the shawl around her shoulders. On the horizon, the first patches of light began to change color, turning from a dark, somber gray to a kaleidoscope of reds and oranges. She brought the mug of coffee up to her lips and sighed as the sun began its ascent into the skies.

A bittersweet feeling washed over Lily.

She had seen a lot of sunsets and sunrises since arriving in Provincetown, many of them from the very same spot, but none of them ever felt like this. Since waking up half an hour ago, all Lily had done was replay the conversation with her dad and wonder if she had done the right thing.

A part of her half hoped he would call her back and make amends.

The other part of her knew it wasn't going to unfold like that.

At least not yet.

Eric Taylor was many things, but impulsive and sentimental were not among them. Having gone her whole life tiptoeing around his rules and trying to reconcile herself to his short-sighted and domineering ways, Lily had no idea what happened next. Her father had always been in the shadows since before she could remember, and even when she stopped coming home for Christmases and holidays, he had still been there, impatient and eager to swoop in.

Had she been too hasty in her decision?

Was there still a way for them to be in each other's lives?

Lily took another long sip of her coffee, the hot liquid burning a path down her throat before it settled in the pit of her stomach. Then she shifted from one foot to the other and sighed. While she hated to admit it, deep down, she had known her father was never going to be okay with her moving out here. Since he had spent her entire life lying to her and carefully cultivating a false image of her mother as nothing but a negligent, unfeeling woman, who hadn't thought twice about leaving her behind, she wasn't sure why it hurt so much to know he didn't approve.

She had, after all, known it was coming.

Yet, she'd still spent the night tossing and turning and listening for the sounds of her children's breathing through the walls. In the dead of night, she'd even checked in on them, taking some comfort from seeing them there, fast asleep and unburdened by the world. Unable to sit still, she'd even crept downstairs and ran into her aunt Ashley in the kitchen, heating up some warm milk.

In silence, the two of them had sat opposite each other at the counter and sipped on their drinks. Unfortunately, Aunt Ashley had long since gone back to sleep, leaving Lily alone to the mercy of her thoughts. She took another long sip, took her phone out of her pocket, and brought it up to her face. As the world around her shifted and came to life, a flock of birds calling out to each other in the distance, she studied her father's name, the last phone call she made.

For too long, she stood there, contemplating what it would be like to call him and walk back on her decision. With a slight shake of her head, she shoved the phone back into her pocket and finished off the last of her coffee. She was still studying the horizon, counting out the number of blue clouds, when a pair of footsteps shuffled behind her. Sara materialized next to her, bundled up in a sweater with her feet stuffed into a pair of fuzzy slippers.

She brought her head to rest against Lily's shoulders. "I'm going to miss it here."

Lily used her free hand to squeeze Sara's shoulder. "I'm going to miss having you all here. It's been a great weekend."

Sara sighed. "Are you going to be okay?"

Lily twisted to give her daughter a half smile. "Sweetheart, I don't want you to worry about me. I'll be fine."

Sara turned her head and held her mother's gaze. "You know, it's okay if you aren't. You've been through a lot, Mom. I can't even imagine what it must feel like for you."

Lily cleared her throat. "I've got the three of you. What more could I possibly need?"

Sara stood up straighter. "It's okay to want to start over and find love again. You deserve it, Mom."

Lily raised an eyebrow. "What gave you the idea that I'm looking for love again? Your mom is too old for that now."

As soon as the words left her lips, an image of Ben

came to mind, his head thrown back mid-laugh and sunlight glistening off of his skin.

Sara snorted. "Oh, please. I saw the way you were looking at that guy the other day—the one who works at Aunt Rebecca's inn. Ben, was it?"

Lily set her mug down on the coffee table behind her and clapped her hands together. "I have no idea what you're talking about."

"Uh-huh, sure. Whatever you say, Mom."

Lily drew Sara closer and ushered her inside. "How about I make you something to eat? Since you've got a long trip back."

Sara waved her comment away. "Don't worry about it, Mom. We can pick something up on the road. Lauren and I are driving back together."

Lily opened the refrigerator door and rummaged around, waiting for her blush to recede. "Good."

"You know, I could picture myself moving out here after college."

Lily lifted her head up and stared at her. "Yeah?"

Sara nodded. "Yeah, I mean, I can be a biologist anywhere. I don't know how Jake would feel about it, but I'm pretty sure I could convince him after a few trips. I'll have to get him to fall in love with the place like I did."

Lily took out a few containers and kicked the refrigerator door shut with the back of her leg. "You don't have to move out here on my account."

Sara gave her a half smile and stepped out from behind the counter. "It wouldn't be on your account, don't worry."

"In that case, I hope you make the right decision for yourself."

Lauren appeared in the kitchen, her hair a wild mess

around her face and the holes in her sweatpants evident. "Sara is the queen of bad decisions."

Sara snorted and gave her sister a withering look. "You'd know all about that, Missy. Can't keep a guy around to save her life."

Lauren scowled and poured herself a cup of coffee. "There's a difference between not keeping a guy around because I'm too busy focusing on school and my own life and not being able to."

Sara took out a bowl and cracked a few eggs. "I see no difference."

Lauren took a sip of her coffee before sticking her tongue out at her sister.

Then the two of them burst into laughter, the sound sending another strong wave of emotion through Lily. She took the bowl of eggs from Sara and began to whisk them slowly, as if it was the most important task in the world. Together, the two of them set up the table, setting out some olives, cheese, and bologna. Once they were done, Lauren came to stand next to Lily and wrapped an arm around her shoulders.

"I was thinking of moving out here after school."

"Really?"

"Yeah, when we were in town the other day, we ran into a few people who swear by your methods, and they were really impressed to learn that I want to become a dietician too. Maybe we can even open up a clinic together."

Lily gave her daughter a half smile. "We can definitely talk about it."

"I knew you guys were going to get sentimental," Liam said as soon as he walked in. "You let the town get under your skin, didn't you?"

Sara rolled her eyes. "Oh, please. I overheard you on the phone with Laura yesterday, pitching this place as a wedding destination."

Liam paused to give his sister a withering look. "Hasn't anyone ever told you it's not polite to eavesdrop?"

"Has anyone ever told you it's not polite to lie and make fun of people?"

Liam reached for the pot of coffee and poured the last of it. "I'm not lying."

Lauren patted his back on the way past. "It's okay to like it here. We've both admitted it."

Liam took a long sip of his coffee and blew out a breath. "All right, fine. The place is growing on me, but I don't know if I would actually want to move out here. Laura needs to like it first and see if she can move her business here, and there's also the fact that I'm a criminal lawyer."

Lauren eyed him over the rim of her mug. "You can be a criminal lawyer anywhere, Liam. Don't pretend like you aren't already picturing it."

"Sometimes, I hate having sisters," Liam grumbled in between sips of his coffee.

With a smile, Lily directed her children to help with the rest of breakfast and setting up the table. When Aunt Ashely came into the kitchen, bleary-eyed and with wrinkled clothing, they were all sitting down at the dining table. Lily kept glancing up from her plate to look around the table and smile.

She blinked back the tears of joy burning the backs of her eyes, not wanting to turn into an emotional mess again.

Once they were done and they helped her clean up, they all disappeared into their rooms to change. Aunt

Ashley left first, lingering during her hugs and pausing to pat Lily's back. With one last smile, she got into her car and drove off, turning into a speck in the distance. As soon as she disappeared, Liam pulled them all in for a hug, and Lily squeezed her eyes shut.

Her heart felt full when they drew back and piled into two cars. Sara and Lauren got into one, sunglasses already perched on their heads. Liam got into the other and paused to adjust his rearview mirror. Lily lifted a hand up to wave at them. She stood on the sidewalk, waving at her children until she couldn't see them anymore. Until her hand hurt, and the tears were spilling freely down her cheeks.

When she couldn't wave anymore, she heaved a sigh and trudged back inside. The door clicked shut behind her, plunging her into silence. She wandered into the living room, absentmindedly picking up and setting down several things. Then she found herself at the foot of the stairs, studying the pictures lined up against the wall. As usual, she stopped at her mother's picture, and the ache in her chest only grew.

She pressed her mouth to the picture and swallowed.

Slowly, she made her way back upstairs and into her room. There, she kicked off her shoes and left them by the door. Her body felt heavy and lethargic as she pulled back the covers and crawled in between them. She flipped onto her side, tucked her hands underneath her head, and stared at the window. For a while, all she could hear was the pounding of her own heart, loud and familiar in her ears.

Little by little, her body grew slack and relaxed as sleep hovered on the edge of her vision. She set her phone down on the nightstand, squeezed her eyes shut, and exhaled.

Sleep came for her shortly after, and all of her dreams were of her life in Provincetown, surrounded by the family she'd found there.

Chapter Twenty-Four

Ben ran a hand through his hair and expelled a breath. "I know it's a big ask, but I really need your help on this."

Lily shifted from one foot to the other and pushed the door open. "Would you like to come in? I just made myself some chamomile tea."

Ben nodded and ducked his head.

Inside, he followed her into the kitchen and hovered near the edge of the counter. She took out another mug, placed the tea bag inside, and waited till the kettle whistled. Then she poured a generous amount of water into both mugs and motioned to Ben, who wordlessly followed her onto the back porch. Carefully, she set his mug down and lowered herself onto the chair.

"Olive talked to Grace, and she agreed to meet with me in an hour," Ben said, the words tumbling out of him in a rush. "I've been up all night trying to think about what to tell her and where to start, but I have no idea how to do this."

Lily sipped her drink. "Just be honest with her, Ben.

She'll appreciate you owning up to your mistakes, trust me."

Ben frowned. "Shouldn't I be trying to get her to understand my side?"

"That's a part of it, sure, but it's not all of it. You need to show her you're sorry, not just tell her."

Ben stared down at his drink, a furrow appearing between his brows. "Olive is going to be there, sitting nearby for moral support."

"That's good."

Ben lifted his gaze up to hers. "I'd like you to be there too, if you don't mind."

Lily took another sip of her drink, heart thudding erratically inside of her chest. "Let me finish my tea, and I'll change."

Ben sipped on his drink and kept sneaking glances at her. "I really appreciate you doing this."

When they were done, Lily crept upstairs and changed into a pair of jeans and a T-shirt. After dragging a brush through her hair, she hurried back downstairs, where Ben lingered near the door. Together, they walked into town, headed directly for the Herring Cove Café.

Olive was already waiting inside at a table near the window. Wordlessly, Lily pulled out her seat and cleared her throat. A short while later, a young, dark-haired woman with hazel eyes and a defiant set of her chin walked in. She glanced around, and her eyes landed on Ben, who sat a few feet away. Lily stiffened and leaned forward in her seat, catching the tense and awkward exchange between them.

As soon as she sat down, Ben sat up straighter and cleared his throat. "Thanks for coming."

Grace Vasquez curled her fingers around her mug

and averted her gaze. "To be honest, I wasn't sure if I was going to."

"I'm glad you did," Ben replied with an exhale. "I've thought about this for years. I even wrote out what I would say to you if I ever got the chance."

Silence stretched between them.

"I'm sorry, Grace," Ben began with a solemn expression. "After the divorce, I should've done better. You know how much I loved your mother and how hard it was for me to accept we weren't good for each other. It's not an excuse. I just wanted you to know."

Grace lifted her gaze up and frowned. "You made me feel like you only cared about me because of her, like I could only talk to you because I was her daughter."

Ben's hand darted out, and he placed it over Grace's. "That couldn't be further from the truth. I know I've got a lot to make up for and a lot that I need to do to prove myself to you, but I've always loved you, Gracie."

Ben paused and swallowed. "I'm sorry I made you feel like that wasn't the case. I'll make it up to you, I promise. If you give me a chance, I'll be the father you deserve."

Grace gave him a small, half smile. "I'd really, really like that."

Ben's answering smile made Lily's heart flutter and miss a beat. "Good. I'd like that too. So, tell me everything; what are you up to now? How's school?"

Olive set her drink down and twisted to face Lily. "I guess he didn't need us after all."

"Having moral support always helps," Lily commented, pausing to take a long sip of her tea. "I'm glad it worked out. I should get going."

Olive glanced up at her. "Thanks for coming."

Lily nodded and pushed her chair back with a screech. On the sidewalk, she paused to shove her hands into the pockets of her sweater. She was lost in thought as she walked back home, replaying the love and relief she'd seen play out between the Vasquez family. By the time she made it back to the house, she was so lost in thought she hadn't even realized someone was sitting on her front porch, a bag at her feet.

After a double take, Lily recognized her aunt Evie, who stood up and brushed lint off of her jeans. "I hope it's okay that I just dropped by."

Lily crossed the distance between them and drew her aunt in for a hug. "Of course, it is. Why didn't you tell me you were coming?"

Aunt Evie shrugged as she pulled away. "To be honest, I wasn't even sure I was until I ended up here. It's as beautiful as you described, Lily."

"You should've called me, Auntie. I would've been here sooner," Lily replied, pausing to take her keys out of her pocket and push the door open.

She bent down to carry her aunt's bag and set it down by the door. After a quick tour of the house, Aunt Evie ducked into the guest room downstairs, and Lily stood by the sliding glass doors, a strange feeling in the center of her chest.

Aunt Evie looped her feeble arm through Lily's and peered through the glass. "I have something for you, but first, let's go for a walk."

In silence, Lily led her down the familiar path and in the direction of the beach.

"I'm sorry about what happened during the funeral," Aunt Evie began, her eyes fixed on an unseen spot on the horizon. "I shouldn't have let Eric treat you like that."

"It's not your responsibility to protect me from him, Auntie." Lily came to a stop on the edge of the water and cleared her throat. "He's a grown man. That's on him."

"You know, for the longest time, Eric wouldn't let me anywhere near you without supervision. He said he didn't want you inheriting any of my defeatist mannerisms and he didn't want my weak personality rubbing off on you."

Lily frowned. "That's cruel. He shouldn't have told you those things.

Aunt Evie unlinked her arm and let it fall limply to her side. "No, he shouldn't have, but Eric has always been like this. He's always treated Mae and me like we weren't as good as him, and he found ways to bring us down, no matter what."

Lily touched her aunt's frail-looking shoulder, her chest cracking open at her words. "I'm sorry."

Aunt Evie's lips lifted into a half smile. "Don't be. I've had an entire lifetime to make peace with my brother and what he's really like. I let him bully and criticize me into submission, but I don't want to do it anymore. Seeing how he behaved at the funeral really drove the point home for me."

"It did?"

Aunt Evie turned her gaze to Lily and frowned. "I should've been there for you when you were younger. I had a feeling Eric was doing the same thing to you, but I told myself it was none of my business. I let myself get caught up in my own life and my own petty drama, and I let you down. I'm sorry."

Lily blinked. "Aunt Evie, you have nothing to be sorry for. It's not your fault."

Aune Evie shook her head. "When I lost my precious Alfred, I withdrew from the world and from people, but I shouldn't have done that. Granted, I like my pets better than I like people, but it's not an excuse."

"Pets can be better than people," Lily agreed in a quiet voice.

"They can be, but that's not the point. The point is that it's time Eric and his manipulation took a back seat. I don't care about keeping the peace anymore, or what he says about me, or how mad he gets; I should've done this years ago."

Lily brought her head to rest against her aunt's shoulder. "You don't have to do all of this, Auntie."

Aunt Evie patted her head. "I want to. It's been a long time coming, trust me. Whiskers, Pigeon, and I all agree that this is the right thing to do."

"Where are the little fur balls anyway?"

"A pet boarding facility in town," Aunt Evie replied with a sigh. "I wasn't sure if you'd be okay with them staying here."

"Of course, I would be." Lily drew back to look at Aunt Evie and smiled. "I'd be happy to have you all here."

Aunt Evie smiled and fell silent.

Later, when they walked back to the house, Aunt Eve's footsteps were lighter and full of purpose. Back at the house, Aunt Evie disappeared into the room and returned with a sealed box. She opened it, revealing pictures, letters, and memorabilia from Lily's childhood, all of them carefully tucked away and preserved by her aunt Mae. One by one, Aunt Evie took the stuff out and laid them down on the counter, taking her time with the explanation as she did.

"When Kelly left, she couldn't take much with her, so these are the few things she had to remember you by, and Aunt Mae sent her a few more the following year. Aunt

Mae left this for me. When I found it a few days ago, I knew I had to bring it here to you," Aunt Evie told her, her voice thick with emotion.

Lily traced her fingers over a worn-out teddy bear. "I can't believe they kept all of these. I don't even remember half of them."

Aunt Evie sniffed. "Your aunt Mae was sentimental like that. Kelly appreciated it though, and there are a few more letters here from your mother."

Lily took the stack, and her heart grew heavy with grief and yearning. "I wish I'd gotten the chance to see this sooner."

"Mae planned on showing it to you when she came to visit before the...before she was taken from us."

Lily pulled her aunt in for a hug and sniffed.

Together, the two of them cried and remembered Aunt Mae. When they were done, Aunt Evie retired to her room, and Lily was left rummaging through the box, feeling closer to her mother than she ever had before. Then she retrieved a jacket from upstairs and went for a walk along the beach, spotting Ben's outline easily.

"If I keep running into you here, I'm going to start thinking you're stalking me," Ben said without looking at her. "Thanks for coming today, by the way."

"You're welcome."

"Life's strange, isn't it? I didn't think I was going to get a second chance with my daughter, but here we are."

"I didn't think I was going to start over in Province-town," Lily added. "We have to make the most of our second chances though."

Ben brushed his hand against hers and exhaled. "We should. So, there's a rumor going around that you've decided to stay in Provincetown."

Lily twisted to face him, a smile hovering on the edge of her lips. "You shouldn't believe everything you hear."

Ben's expression dimmed. "Does that mean you're not staying?"

Lily smiled. "No, I am, but you still shouldn't listen to rumors."

Ben laced his fingers through hers and grinned.

A jolt of electricity raced up her arm.

Hand in hand, they walked along the edge of the water, with Lily drawing closer and closer to Ben, the comforting smell of him washing over her. During the walk, his grip on her hand tightened, and she found that she didn't mind.

She liked holding hands with him.

Chapter Twenty-Five

After a long walk, Lily's heart was still racing, and the butterflies in her stomach hadn't abated. In silence, Ben walked her back to the house and climbed up the stairs to the front porch. Underneath the light of the moon, he framed her face in his hands and hesitated.

She looked into his eyes, held her breath, and waited.

A heartbeat later, his lips touched hers, and something in her exploded and unfurled. She made a low whimpering sound and melted against him, her fingers coming up around his neck. Then she threaded them through his hair and sighed. Ben smiled into the kiss, tasting like mint mouthwash and watermelon gum.

It was a heady combination that made her head spin.

She clutched him tighter and inhaled, the scent of Old Spice and sandalwood wafting up her nostrils and making her stomach tighten. All too soon, Ben drew back and pressed his forehead against hers. Over the pounding of her heart, she listened for the sound of his uneven breathing, a smile hovering on the edge of her lips. When he opened his eyes to look at her, and she saw the depth of emotion in his eyes, from hope to understanding and everything in between, her stomach did an odd little flip.

Lily realized two things at the same time.

Coming to Provincetown was one of the best decisions she ever made.

And she was crazy about Ben Vasquez.

Ben brushed his lips against hers and chuckled. "I think we have an audience. Is that one of your relatives?"

Lily glanced over her shoulders and saw the curtain swish back into place. "That would be my aunt Evie."

"Ah." Ben released her and took a step back. He cupped his hands over his mouth and raised his voice. "It's nice to meet you, Aunt Evie. This is not how I pictured meeting more of Lily's family members."

Lily giggled and slapped his arm. "Don't encourage her."

"She's probably already informed the rest of the family," Ben told her with a grin. "By this time tomorrow, we'll be the talk of the town."

"How can you be so calm about it?"

Ben shrugged. "You get used to it. Besides, they'll move on to something else eventually."

"I'm not sure I share your confidence."

Ben gave her another kiss that made her toes curl and her head spin. She tilted forward, and Ben caught her, pausing to set her back on her feet. Once he was sure she was steady, he gave her a quick hug and disappeared down the path. With a smile, Lily walked back into the house and heard the door to the guest room click shut. She shook her head and smiled.

In the morning, when her kids all joined in on a conference call, she could tell Aunt Evie had spilled the beans because of how they tiptoed around the subject of Ben and the knowing looks they kept giving her. As soon as the call ended, she set the phone down on the kitchen counter and pulled out one of the high stools. She sat down, tossed her hair over her shoulder, and studied her aunt's back.

"All right, just get it off your chest already."

Aunt Evie spun around to face her, weathered face looking a little too innocent. "I have no idea what you're talking about."

"I know you were spying on Ben and me, and I know you told the kids."

Aunt Evie untied her apron and grimaced. "I couldn't help myself. I wanted to be sure you were okay after what I showed you...and the kids already had their suspicions. I told them I can't confirm anything."

Lily laughed. "That's as good as a confession."

Aunt Evie draped the apron over the back of a chair and carried a pan over, pausing to set it down over the trivet. "I can call them back if you want."

"It's okay, Auntie."

Aunt Evie cleared her throat. "I know it's a lot to ask, but I was thinking I could stay here for a bit while I figured out my next move. You know how lonely I've been since Alfred passed, and I think Provincetown is exactly what I need to start over."

"What about Dad? He's not going to be happy once he hears about this."

Aunt Evie pulled out a fork and knife to cut through the omelet. "Your father will get over it. There's nothing in New York for me, anyway. There hasn't been for a while. You and I, on the other hand, have a lot of catching up to do."

"We do?"

Aunt Evie smiled at her. "If you'll have me."

Lily picked up her own fork and swallowed past the lump in her throat. "I would love to have you, Auntie. You're welcome to stay for as long as you need."

"I'll need to make arrangements to sell the apartment in New York," Aunt Evie told her with a frown. "But I was thinking I could eventually buy something here, maybe a nice cottage somewhere."

"I know a few people who can help with that," Lily offered in between bites of food. "Grandma Jen and Grandpa Frank haven't gone back to Falmouth yet. They're staying with Aunt Heather. Would you like to meet them?"

"Sweetheart, I would love to."

"I'll give them a call after breakfast."

An hour later, after they were finished tidying up, the doorbell rang, and Lily's grandparents came in, beaming and dressed identically in their khakis and shirts. Grandma Jen's wrinkled face split into a grin when she saw Aunt Evie. She drew her in for a hug, and the three of them sat down on the couch together. Before she could close the door, Lily spotted her aunts in the distance, walking arm in arm and sporting smiles.

In the doorway, they greeted her and smiled.

Suddenly, the five of them were in the living room, sharing stories and laughing. Aunt Evie sat in the center; face flushed with pleasure as she entertained them all with stories about Lily's childhood. The four of them fell silent as they listened intently, hanging on to Aunt Evie's every word. Like it was the most important thing in the world.

Lily couldn't tell if she was embarrassed or pleased.

All she knew was she was happy Aunt Evie had been there, offering a bridge between the two worlds and telling stories Lily couldn't remember. A few hours later, when all three of her children joined her on a Zoom call, with Jake and Laura in the background, Lily couldn't have been more thrilled.

She set the laptop down on the coffee table in the living room, and five pairs of eyes turned to the screen. Lauren sat at her desk, a pile of books next to her and a questionable stain in the center of her sweater. Sara was in the kitchen stirring something in a pot while Jake came in and out of the kitchen, and Liam was on the treadmill, dark hair matted to his forehead, and Laura's face emerging now and again, tight with focus.

"We made our own family tree," Lauren announced, pausing to prop her phone up against the wall. "It's not as impressive as Mom's family tree sheet, but it's been helping us learn everybody's names."

"And how we're all related," Sara added over her shoulders. "We've even color-coded it."

"I thought the family tree sheet was meant to be a secret," Aunt Heather said with a smile. "Not that I think there's anything wrong with that."

"Are we going to be adding another name to the list soon?"

Several pairs of eyes turned to Lily expectantly.

"Can't a woman have any privacy in this family?" Lily rose to her feet and ducked into the kitchen to hide her blush. "Ben and I are just getting to know each other, that's all."

Ben's head poked out from behind the door. "I heard my name. What did I do now?"

Lily's hand flew to her chest. "How did you get here?"

"The door was open," Ben replied. "Can I come in?"

Lily's hand moved to her hair. "Yeah, of course."

Ben stepped in, kicked the door shut behind him, and produced a bouquet of daisies he'd been holding behind his back. "I got you these."

Laughter erupted throughout the room.

"I wasn't aware we had an audience." Ben glanced over at her aunts, pressed together on one couch, and his eyes lingered on her grandparents on the smaller couch. He waved at Lily's kids on the screen and swung his gaze back to hers. She smiled, stepped forward, and took the bouquet of flowers out of his hand.

He gave her a quick peck on the cheek and laced his fingers through hers.

"I didn't mean to interrupt," Ben began with an apologetic smile. "I just wanted to stop by."

"Yes, you weren't interrupting at all. I was just telling them stories about how Lily used to wear the diaper on her head like a hat."

Lily's mouth fell open. "Aunt Evie, you told me you were going to stop telling that story in public."

"I'm sorry, sweetheart, but you were so cute." Aunt Evie stood up and grabbed her purse off the counter. "I've got a few pictures here somewhere, and I think I've got a few videos of her when she pretended to be Wonder Woman."

Ben draped an arm over her waist. "I bet she was a cute Wonder Woman."

Aunt Evie settled back onto the couch and scrolled through her phone. "She really was, and she had a phase where she boycotted deodorant because she thought it was too girly."

"Ben and I are going for a walk," Lily announced a

little too loudly. "I don't think I can stick around and listen to this."

In spite of his protests, she marched him out and in the direction of the beach. He spent the entire walk poking fun at her and teasing her. She waded, ankle-deep into the water, and splashed him. Ben threw her over his shoulders and spun in circles till they both fell face-first into the sand. Breathless and giddy, Lily raced Ben back into the house, where they snuck upstairs, kissing and laughing the whole time.

When they came back down, someone had started the fire, the flames dancing and leaping as they cast shadows across the walls. Ben hadn't let go of her hand once, even when she went into the kitchen to hunt down some snacks and drinks. Hours later, the conversation was still in full swing when the doorbell rang, and Ben went to answer it.

Olive and Grace stood on the other side of the door.

Grace threw her arms around her father when she saw him. He glanced at Lily over his shoulder and ushered his daughter inside in the direction of the empty dining table. Olive offered her a small smile on the way past. Lily was about to make her way over to them when her phone rang, slicing through the air. She snatched it off the table behind the door and pressed it to her ear.

Amy's voice sounded garbled, like she was underwater.

Lily's brows furrowed together as she hung up and dialed her again.

On the fourth ring, it went straight to voicemail.

With a frown, Lily hung up and tried again, only this time, the phone disconnected. She ran a hand over her face, lead settling in the center of her stomach. Then the doorbell rang, bringing her back to the present with a jolt. Lily tried dialing her stepmother again and used her free hand to open the door.

The phone nearly fell out of her hand when she realized that none other than Amy Gruntle, her stepmother, stood on her doorstep. She had a small bag next to her, red hair gathered into a bun on top of her head, and clothes that looked wrinkled and slept in.

As soon as Lily's eyes traveled up, Amy offered her a tight smile and pulled her in for a hug. Lily's arms came up around her stepmother, and she ushered her in, pausing to motion to Aunt Heather, who hurried over and brought her bag in. In silence, Lily led Amy to the room next to Aunt Evie's and left her on the bed.

"Not that I'm not thrilled to have you here, but what are you doing here? Are you okay?"

Amy avoided her gaze. "Your father is away on a business trip, so I thought I'd come down here and see what all the fuss is about."

Lily beamed as she sat down next to her stepmother and draped an arm over her shoulders. "I'm so glad you decided to come. You have no idea how happy I am to have you here."

Amy cleared her throat and offered Lily another tight smile, her eyes still darting all over the room. "It looks different than I expected. I hope it's okay I showed up unannounced."

Lily squeezed her shoulders. "Of course, it is. I've got room. How long did you say Dad was going to be away for?"

Amy froze. "I didn't, why?"

Lily stood and let her eyes sweep over Amy. "You've got a big bag, so I was just wondering..."

Amy wrung her fingers together and took an unsteady step back. "Oh, I'm not sure yet. He might be extending his trip... We haven't spoken much since he left, so..."

Lily's stomach dipped, and she offered Amy a small smile. "It's okay, anyway. You're welcome to stay as long as you'd like."

Whatever the real reason was, Lily didn't care.

Lily had a feeling it had nothing at all to do with a spontaneous trip down to Provincetown and everything to do with the letters they'd been exchanging. But she wasn't going to push Amy to talk about it, not yet.

"I'll let you freshen up. Come out whenever you're ready." Lily gave Amy another smile and lingered in the doorway.

When Amy started to unpack, still avoiding Lily's gaze as she did, Lily sighed.

As soon as she stepped back outside, laughter and conversation rising through the air, she couldn't help but glance over at Ben. He was patting his daughter's back and murmuring to her, but he looked up, and when their eyes met, he smiled. A moment later, he glanced away, and Lily went to sit next to her grandparents.

She had no idea what would happen from here on out or why her stepmother was in the next room, but she was sure it would only be a matter of time before she did.

All she knew was she felt incredibly lucky to have her family and Ben by her side, regardless of where life took her or how things unfolded.

And for the first time in a long time, she wasn't afraid of the future.

Because it was all hers for the taking.

Coming Next from Kimberly

Pre Order Falmouth Echoes

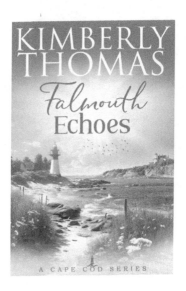

Other Books by Kimberly

The Archer Inn

An Oak Harbor Series

A Yuletide Creek Series

A Festive Christmas Series

A Cape Cod Series

Made in United States
Cleveland, OH
08 February 2025

14102648R00128